NIAMH TAKES ULYSSES HOME

Mary Rochford was born and grew up in Dublin. She has spent most of her adult life in Birmingham, England, where she read English and History at the University of Birmingham. She obtained a Masters in Literary Studies at Birmingham City University and has worked as a lecturer in Further Education. Her collection of short stories, *Gilded Shadows*, was long listed for the Frank O'Connor International Short Story Award and won Birmingham City Library Readers' Book for Birmingham Award.

Mary Rochford

NIAMH TAKES ULYSSES HOME

Tia Publishing

First Published by Tia Publishing 2010
37 Chesterwood Road
Birmingham
B13 0QG

Copyright © Mary Rochford 2010

This book is sold subject to the condition that it shall not by way of trade or otherwise, be lent, resold, hired out, or otherwise circulated without the publisher's prior consent in any form of binding or cover other than that in which it is published and without a similar condition including this condition being imposed on the subsequent purchaser.

All characters and events in this publication, other than those clearly in the public domain, are fictitious and any resemblance to real persons, living or dead, is purely coincidental.

ISBN 978-0-9557810-1-8

PEFC Certified
This product is from sustainably managed forests and controlled sources
www.pefc.org
PEFC/16-33-415

Mixed Sources
Product group from well-managed forests, and other controlled sources
www.fsc.org Cert no. TT-COC-002641
© 1996 Forest Stewardship Council

Printed by: Print On Demand Worldwide
9 Culley Court
Bakewell Road
Orton Southgate
Peterborough
PE2 6XD

Also by Mary Rochford

GILDED SHADOWS

GILDED SHADOWS

'A lovely piece of writing…a very sure touch.'
Mary Kenny
Author, journalist, broadcaster.

'Reveals an acutely observant eye for the intricacies of human relationships, the subtleties of language and people's intriguing manipulation of past and present…Guardian Angel is a moving tale which subtly tackles our preconceptions about race, foreigners and the unexpected kindness of strangers.'
Irish World

'The landscapes of the South of France —cosmopolitan Nice, the opulence of Monaco, the beautiful hill village of Eze — are an integral part of the [final] story, adding depth and texture.'
UC Magazine

'The breadth of characters featured makes this collection accessible and enjoyable to all readers.'
The Harp

'A collection of intriguing tales…the urban landscape of Birmingham is paid as much attention as the wild seascapes of rural Ireland or the bright prettiness of the South of France.'
Liz Broomfield bookcrossing.com

For my mother and father

Game on: Returned Exile versus Native City.

But she wasn't acquainted with the entire city knew only the Southside intimately had never really known the Northside even when she'd lived here and traipsing round the Southside would be challenging enough so probably fairer to say Returned Exile versus Personal Demons.

Right.

*

The flutter of apprehension that started in the pit of her stomach rose to her throat and found release in a deep sigh. Fear mounted a further attack and she made herself take deep breaths: this trip had, after all, been her call. But she had come prepared, had devised a strategy that should ease the way.

So no need for panic.

The idea had come to her as she had tried for the umpteenth time to finish reading James Joyce's *Ulysses*. She had decided she would traverse the city, not in one day as Bloom had done — she wasn't fit enough for that — and unlike Joyce she was not concerned with literary unities. She would allow herself a week in which to visit all the places she wanted to see and she would take the masterpiece of a fellow Dubliner with her and finish reading it while she was there. And she might do some research. An idea had been rattling round her head for some months and this could be the time to pin it down.

A good plan?

Couldn't be bettered.

Several birds with one stone.

*

The wing of the plane glinted in the sun as it burst through a mist of grey cloud. Far below the Irish Sea lapped the sandy beaches of North Dublin. The plane came in low over the choppy green water and Niamh prepared herself for the jolt of landing.

The plane hit the runway with a juddering bump and taxied towards the terminal. Niamh* stayed in her seat until the other passengers disembarked. Hesitating at the door of the aircraft, she looked beyond the busy scene of the airport to the green fields that had, so far, escaped the developers. She breathed deeply, wanting to fill her lungs with fresh Irish air. The sting of diesel caught at her throat and she was racked by a bout of coughing.

"Can I be of assistance, madam." The steward smiled, his eyes blank with indifference. Niamh shook her head, grabbed hold of the rail to steady herself and started her descent.

*

The express bus took her, in record time, through the recently opened Dublin Port Tunnel and onto the quayside in the city centre.

The tunnel had taken five long years to complete and had encountered many mishaps along the way. Dubliners hadn't wasted this golden opportunity to

* Neave

show off their greatest talent — the propensity to vilify their own. On a previous visit a bus driver had explained the situation to Niamh. "The concrete used was sub-standard so the tunnel leaks like a sieve. Ah, but there's nothin' to worry about missus. Doesn't it make perfect economic sense to ensure that everything built in Ireland is substandard, and for two very good reasons: one, all the re-builds keep the Celtic Tiger roaring and two, doesn't it help our lords and masters in Leinster House and their business cronies make an honest buck?"

To speed the entire process the tunnel was built in two sections, one starting at the port, the other close to the airport. Reliable sources whispered that the two sections were off-course and would not meet in the middle.

"Surely that can't be true?" Niamh had asked the bus-driver as he negotiated the chaos of the building site. "Surely it's a joke? Modern technology would make mistakes like that impossible."

"Ah, don't mind them missus," the driver said, taking his eyes off the road and winking at Niamh. "Sure we've nothing to worry about. This is Ireland: all we need is a miracle and the archbishop has called for a weekend of prayer and abstinence from alcohol and sex to help the matter along. So there's no problem. We're home and dry, if you'll pardon the pun."

The advantages of the tunnel were lost as they reached the quayside. The bus inched its way through choking traffic along North West Quay towards O'Connell Bridge. From her vantage point on the upper deck, Niamh looked out on Dublin as it adjusted to a new day. Squawking gulls circled the swaying masts of a dozen sailing boats that lined the quayside, their crews nowhere in sight. Here and there people hurried along the riverside path, while others strolled in the morning sun.

Twenty minutes later they reached Custom House Quay and Rowan Gillespie's bronze statues that commemorated the starving masses that had fled Ireland for America during the nineteenth century. The elongated figures, emaciated and ghost-like, looked towards the heavens in silent supplication, clutching tiny bundles to their sunken chests. As the sculptures weathered and aged, yellow scale covered the pitiful group like flakes of festering skin.

It was a hot sunny afternoon. Niamh was fourteen years old, her frame generously padded with puppy fat, her flaming red hair a scouring pad of tangled curls. She was walking along the cobbled wharf opposite Custom House Quay, linking arms with her pal Philomena Reilly. Philomena was tall and skinny. At a time when height in women was not favoured she walked with a stoop and kept her head down. She frequently bumped into other pedestrians and the occasional lamppost.

It was Saturday and they had begged their mothers to be allowed to take the bus into O'Connell Street and look at the shops in Henry Street. Permission granted. But on the understanding that they would alight at The Pillar, visit Arnott's and Roche's Stores, buy ice-creams in Woolworth's, cross over O'Connell Street and catch a number fourteen or fifteen bus outside Cleary's. Their curfew was four o'clock. Sharp.

Initially they stuck to the plan. They gasped and giggled their way around the different departments of both stores, savoured the creamy delights of Woollies' ice-cream, enjoyed being part of the heaving throng.

On this Saturday the usual crowd of weekend shoppers was augmented by dozens of handsome American sailors: the dazzling white of their uniforms accentuating taut muscular frames and smooth tanned complexions.

"The fleet's in. Did ya, see tha'? The fleet's in; the Yanks are in town." A young woman standing next to Niamh as they queued for ice cream nudged her friend, her face flushed with excitement. "Janey Mack, Imelda, Dublin will be leppin' this week-end."

The fleet had arrived in town the previous evening for a stay of three days so the women of Dublin needed to be quick off the mark. The women of Dublin proved up to the task. They strolled along O'Connell Street, dressed to kill in brightly coloured circular skirts that swirled above shapely ankles. Halter necklines exposed soft white flesh. The sultry streets sizzled with barely suppressed lust as local girls clung to their temporary *beaux*, arms linked tightly, eyes gazing in admiration at the young men who could not believe their luck, who had expected a cold reception in Catholic Ireland and who were delighted to have been proved wrong.

Niamh and Philomena stood waiting to cross the wide expanse of Dublin's main thoroughfare. As they licked their melting ice creams they felt a strange sense of unease. The brazen sensuality of the young couples made them blush with embarrassment and they looked away hurriedly. But again and again their gaze was drawn back to the sexually charged scene.

The woman at the bus stop hugged herself in righteous fury, her fat arms folded, providing a shelf for her massive breasts.

"Those trollops should be ashamed of themselves; they're letting themselves down and mortifying respectable Irish women with their wanton behaviour.

I don't think those ships should be allowed to dock at all. They bring nothing but trouble," she said.

"Sure leave the young ones alone; aren't they only having a bit of fun?" a wizened man retorted, taking a last drag on his Woodbine before throwing the butt into the channel.

"I think it's grea' that they visit Dublin," a young woman chipped in. "You can go on board and look round the whole ship and they give you popcorn and chewing gum and it's all for nothin'."

"Where's the ship?" Philomena asked.

*

They had been walking along the deserted quays for almost an hour, but still the huge grey ship that the young woman had described was nowhere in sight.

"She said it would only take fifteen minutes to get there," Niamh moaned. There was no shade by the riverside and the fierce sun belted down, burning her pale freckled skin a deep pink. Sweat streaked Philomena's face and neck; she was thirsty and worried, but she felt compelled to keep going. Although she had said little to persuade Niamh to embark on this reckless jaunt, she felt she'd been the driving force behind it. She had asked the question as to the ship's whereabouts, had cast a challenging look at her friend and nodded in the direction of the river. For a brief moment Niamh had hesitated, but then she strode away from the bus stop and followed Philomena across O'Connell Bridge, left onto Burgh Quay. They kept going until they reached Sir John Rogerson's Quay, but still hadn't arrived at their destination.

Except for the occasional grumble, they stayed silent during the long trek. They knew, without knowing how they knew, that the quays were out of bounds, but still they pressed on. It was not the thought of free popcorn and chewing gum and the opportunity to tour an American ship that drove them. They kept going because they couldn't clear their minds of the image of young sailors holding tightly to laughing excited girls on the airless streets of Dublin. They knew, without knowing what it meant, that they wanted to be one of those girls, wanted to feel a strong arm encircle their waist, wanted to be pressed tightly against a muscular body. They knew this would not happen to them, not on that day, but if they boarded the ship, stood close to a handsome sailor, brushed his fingertips as he offered them chewing gum, that would do — for now. Everything else would follow.

*

"Now what are you lovely young ones doing all the way down here on your own?" The man was surrounded by rays of light that blinded them as they tried to make out his face. He had appeared from nowhere — one minute they were alone by the riverside and the next minute he was standing in front of them, shimmering and indistinct, blocking their path.

"We're looking for the American ship," Philomena was the first to respond.

"Are you sure that's all you're looking for? Sure two pretty girls like yourselves could find more exciting things on the quays than a foreign ship." He moved towards them and his face was suddenly visible. It was greasy and streaked with sweat and his purple lips were parted in an ingratiating smile.

"We're looking for the American ship," Philomena, repeated, taking a step backwards. Her arm rose from her side and she reached, blindly, for Niamh's hand. "We're going on a tour and we're going to get some popcorn and chewing gum. They give it away for nothing."

The man wiped his face with a dirty hanky. He looked at them in silence for what seemed a long time and then he shrugged and said, "Sure isn't the ship closed to the public. No one is allowed on after five o'clock. You young ones should be off home. Your mammies will be wondering where you are."

*

The slap was hard and stinging. Niamh's hand flew to her face and she rocked on her heels, just managing to stay upright. She ducked to avoid the next blow and it caught her on the shoulder.

"I'll give you quays! I'll give you quays! To think a daughter of mine would go traipsing down the quays, gallivanting after American sailors like a cheap trollop!"

"We only wanted to see the ship," Niamh cried.

"I'll give you ship!" Niamh moved quickly to the other side of the kitchen table to avoid the blow that accompanied her mother's scream. "You waltz in here at seven o'clock when I told you to be home for four o'clock sharp. You could have been lying dead in some hospital for all I knew."

Her mother stopped to catch her breath and Niamh inched her way towards the door. "Don't run away from me when I'm talking to you. Do you hear me?

Come back here, this minute. I'll kill you when I get my hands on you."

She'd been confined to the house for a week, forbidden to see Philomena ever again, but the worst part of her punishment was enduring the taunts of her brothers. No matter how often she protested her innocent intent of simply wanting to see the ship, they didn't believe her. They made wet kissing noises and sang,

"All the nice girls love a sailor
All the nice love a tar.
For there's something about a sailor,
For you know what sailors are."

over and over and over again.

Niamh remained in her seat while the bus inched its way into a parking space on Eden Quay and was almost decapitated by an enormous rucksack as a young man heaved it onto his back.

"Sorry, ma'am," he said, his voice loud and cheerful.

"You need to be careful." she replied. "You've got a lethal weapon there."

"Could you tell me where O'Connell Street is, ma'am?"

"Turn left off the bus; take a first right and you're there."

"It's my first trip to Ireland. I'm staying at the Gresham Hotel tonight, picking up a car tomorrow and touring for three days."

"And you plan to see the whole country while you're here?"

"That would be great but I really want to see where my folks came from in County Cork so that's where I'm headed."

She followed him down the stairs and onto the crowded path, almost tripping over her feet as a wave of uncertainty, coupled with nervous excitement, swept over her. Despite the crush on the narrow path she stood still, taking in deep breaths of the fume-laden air, trying to steady herself.

Back in Birmingham her plan had seemed to make sense. She had spent some time compiling a list of places she wanted to visit and plotting her route. She would start and finish her visit in O'Connell Street, following a circular route. The idea of a circular route appealed to her — it promised a gentle progression, a journey without end.

The sensible option was to catch a bus to her hotel in Merrion, check in, drop off her bag and then head back to the city centre.

But she didn't want to go to Merrion. She wanted to start her journey now, to stroll along the city's main thoroughfare, abandon herself to the rhythm and mood of the place, drink in its sights and sounds, inhale its smells, feel the pulse of the dynamic energetic Dublin of the present.

"Hey, you: I've asked you four times now to ge' out of the way so I can ge' past," the irritated voice of a young woman, trying to manoeuvre a child's buggy through the crush of pedestrians, broke through her reverie.

Niamh hauled her rucksack onto her shoulder and walked towards O'Connell Bridge.

*

Daniel O'Connell, cast in stone and impervious to insult or injury, towered above the southern end of the street that bore his name.

Niamh's feelings about the man who had been hailed as a hero and was lauded as The Liberator— the man who was responsible for achieving Catholic Emancipation in 1829 — were ambivalent, which was hardly surprising. Opinion in her family about this giant of Irish history had been divided. Her mother, who came from County Clare where they had defied Westminster and returned him as their member of parliament, thought O'Connell had been a fine figure of a man, loved and cherished by all the poor Catholics of Ireland, whom he had led out of penury and slavery.

Her father felt her mother should learn her history before she opened her gob and made a fool of herself with her ignorant blather. He denounced O'Connell as a priest-licking toady who, as Lord Mayor of Dublin, had set the British army against striking workers. For her father this was the worst mortaler a man could commit. A close second, for a Wexford man like himself, was The Liberator's condemnation of The United Irishmen's uprising of 1789.

"That great hunk of lard was a self-aggrandising, expedient bowsie and don't try to tell me anything different," he would declaim.

"I think he was only gorgeous and I think you're only jealous." Her mother's *coup de grâce* invariably put an end to the shenanigans — until the next time.

*

The man standing next to Niamh, as she waited for the traffic lights to change, obviously belonged to her mother's school of history.

"Youngsters today have no respect at all. If they knew anything about the past, knew what that man had endured for the sake of the people of Ireland, the young buggers wouldn't be clambering all over his statue as though it was a feckin' obstacle course," he spluttered, stabbing his finger at two teenagers who had managed to climb onto the bronze angels guarding the lower level of the memorial. His eyes were red-rimmed and bulging, like blisters ready to pop; specks of foamy spittle settled in the corners of his mouth.

Niamh and the other pedestrians waiting to cross the street moved, almost imperceptibly, away from him.

"Brazen brats that's what they are," he shouted, before throwing himself headlong into the surging traffic.

Niamh closed her eyes, unable to watch his kamikaze weave through buses and taxis. When she looked again he was nowhere in sight. She scanned the pavement opposite, but he had vanished into the dense crowd.

*

She reached the other side of the road and couldn't remember why she had crossed over. She was standing on the corner of Batchelor's Walk and in the distance could see, held aloft by curved ironwork, the three lamps which crowned Ha'penny Bridge.

A smile tugged at her lips. Like most Dubliners she loved that bridge. The only pedestrian walk-way over the Liffey until the Millennium Bridge opened in 1999, it provided a shortcut from Dame Street through to the central shopping area of Abbey Street, Mary Street, Henry Street and — the jewel in Dublin's crown for those who wanted fruit, veg and a knock-about, roustabout verbal exchange with the stall-holders — Moore Street.

*

She glanced at her watch. It was almost eleven o'clock and she was hungry and the day was heating up.

She had left Birmingham in the chill of early morning and had dressed accordingly. Now that there was warmth in the October sun she was too hot and she was feeling slightly queasy. She needed to sit down, needed to eat and needed to divest herself of her fleecy jacket.

She was spoilt for choice. She could stroll up O'Connell Street and choose one of the many coffee bars or cafés; she could amble along the river to Ormond Quay, struggle up the wonky stairs of The Winding Stair Café and enjoy a coffee and cake while watching the world go by or she could make a dash for Bewley's in Grafton Street and devour one of their Irish breakfasts.

Her stomach won out. With a wistful glance at the three lamps she launched herself into the traffic, walked briskly across O'Connell Bridge, along Westmoreland Street, past the Bank of Ireland and up Grafton Street.

All her life she'd had a problem with fainting: collapsing like a felled tree, coming round a few minutes later, looking up into a circle of contorted faces.

Her earliest memory of this unfortunate propensity was the day of her first holy communion. But she must have started her swooning before that. Why else would she have worried as she walked down the central aisle of The Church of Mary Immaculate Refuge of Sinners, togged out as a miniature bride, that the blood might seep slowly from her head to her feet, that she would be thrown off-balance, that her legs would wobble, that she would sink to the ground? Worse still she might topple over without any of the warning signs and hit the floor with a great wallop, cracking her head open and bleeding to death in the church right there in front of the parish priest, Sister Scholastica, her fellow communicants, her mammy and daddy and her sniggering brothers.

*

Sister Scholastica had spent months preparing them for the auspicious day. But before they could receive the body and blood of Christ they had to survive the ordeal of their first confession. They had to learn their catechism off by heart, learn how to say, "Bless me father for I have sinned; this is my first confession," without making a mistake, list all their sins and say an act of contrition. Niamh had mastered numbers one, two and four of these requirements without difficulty, but had hit a brick wall with number three.

"Intent is a significant factor in sinning," Sister Scholastica said, her voice clear and sharp as steel. She stood limbless and erect; a rigid black column in her floor-length habit, hands folded beneath the cape that fell from her shoulders to her waist. "If we intend to do bad deeds then we commit sin," she continued, "and with every sin we drive a nail into the flesh of Christ just as the Romans did when they crucified him."

Niamh couldn't figure it out. She knew that disobeying her mammy and daddy was a sin, but she wasn't sure about intent. Sometimes she didn't know she'd been disobedient until after the event; it wasn't always easy to know what grown-ups expected. She didn't intend losing her temper, but when her brothers jumped out at her from a hiding place or when they diverted her attention so that they could steal her sweets a red mist descended and she lashed out with hands and feet in a vain attempt to inflict pain. At such times, without an exercise of deliberate will, bad words sprang from her mouth.

*

She sat with her classmates on the long wooden pew and as each one entered the dark interior of the confession-box the remaining children moved along. Sister Scholastica had organized them in alphabetical order so Niamh could not sit next to her best school-friend, Cathleen Byrne. She had to wait a long time and her terror grew as she inched nearer and nearer. At last it was her turn.

She stepped into the dark coffin-like confessional and the door closed with a thump. Blindly, she fumbled until her hands found the smooth wood of the kneeler. She knelt down and her chest was heaving, her lungs begging for air. She jumped as a wooden slat was pushed back, sending a shaft of light into the confined space. A shadowy figure towered above her.

"What sins have you committed, my child?" the priest asked, his voice hoarse and thick.

Niamh made the sign of the cross and whispered her prepared list. "I disobeyed my mammy and daddy three times. I lost my temper four times. I said bad words twice." She recited an act of contrition, listened for her penance and, in her haste to escape, stumbled and fell into the aisle. Her clumsiness earned her a flinty look from Sister Scholastica, but she didn't notice. She breathed deeply again and again filling her lungs with the dusty air of the church, knelt down and said a penance of one Our Father and one Hail Mary.

She should have felt relieved and happy that she was now pure and free from sin, but she had an uneasy feeling that editing the list of her sins was itself a sin. She had reduced the number and kind of her misdemeanours, had done it to show herself in a good light. This was an act of pride and she had done it intentionally and had driven another nail into the flesh of Jesus Christ and the next day she would receive her first holy communion in a state of sin and that would be another sin — a mortal one — and if she died in a state of mortal sin she would go to hell where she would burn for eternity and never see the face of god.

*

The silver light of May sunshine woke her early next morning. Her mouth was dry and her stomach ached with hunger, but she could do nothing to relieve her discomfort.

"The Church dictates that you fast from midnight before receiving communion," Sister Scholastica said, her face scrunched into pug-like folds by the rigid wimple of the St. Louis Order. "We must cleanse our bodies as well as our souls before receiving Christ. We do this by abstinence from food and drink."

On a hanger to her right, a dress of white organza, liberally sprinkled with pearls and sequins, shone and sparkled. Niamh gazed at it with a *frisson* of delight: she loved the satin Peter Pan collar, the tiny pearl buttons that ran from neck to waistline and the satin sash which tied in a large bow to the back. A circular veil and a tiara of pearls hung next to the dress. A bead bag and white gloves were placed on a nearby chair and a pair of white buckskin shoes stood pert and expectant on the floor beneath.

"I aim this warning mainly at the girls," Sister Scholastica said, swivelling her head from side to side, spraying the class with steely looks. "But I want the boys to beware as well. Making your first holy communion is a blessed sacrament, not an occasion for the sin of pride. Communicants wear their best clothes to show respect for God, not to show themselves off. Remember that."

As she looked longingly at the outfit she would wear in a couple of hours a pang of anxiety gripped Niamh's heart. In delighting at the prospect of swanking in her new clothes she had committed another sin.

*

She walked down the central aisle of the church accompanied by a young boy dressed in a dark suit and sporting a large white rosette on his lapel. From behind and above, the voices of the choir rose and swelled in encouragement.

> Soul of my saviour,
> Sanctify my breast,
> Bo-dy of Chr-i-i-st
> Be thou my sav-ing guest
> Blood of my Sav-i-our,
> Bathe me in thy tide,
> Wa-sh me ye waters,
> Streaming from his side.

Niamh was starving and she felt faint, but she fought off the feeling of nausea. She knelt at the altar, opened her mouth and received the body of Christ. Walking with bowed head she returned to her seat, trying desperately to swallow the tiny disc, but it had lodged in the roof of her parched mouth and would not budge.

"Do not allow the body of our Saviour to touch your teeth," the parish priest had urged when he visited the school. "Don't chew it and don't let it melt in your mouth."

Niamh had reached her pew and she was still struggling with the problem of how to rid herself of the blessed host in an acceptable manner. She placed her tongue at the back of her throat and attempted to dislodge it, to prise it free. Her stomach and throat muscles convulsed, causing her to heave. She coughed and the tiny sphere of unleavened bread shot from her mouth and flew across the floor.

Sister Scholastica was on her feet. She towered above Niamh, the tight wimple squeezing the swollen globe of her face until it seemed it might explode. Her hand shot out and she grabbed Niamh's arm.

Mercifully, the blood drained from Niamh's head, her legs buckled and she fell forward.

I'll have sausage — well done, bacon, egg, tomato and …"

"Yes, yes, full Irish breakfast." The Chinese waitress nodded and smiled.

"No, no, just the …"

"Full Irish breakfast," the waitress repeated.

In the end they used a rudimentary sign language: Niamh pointed to the items on the menu she wished to order and the young woman smiled and nodded vigorously in agreement.

Niamh looked around the large space. She was glad to be here, pleased that Bewley's still existed. A few years previously she'd hurried from the airport bus which had dropped her in O'Connell Street, dashed along Grafton Street, rushed into the building, hoping to be in time for breakfast, to find that the restaurant entrance had been blocked off.

"What's going on?" she had demanded of the assistant who was serving coffee and cakes in the café that opened onto the street.

"The restaurant's closed," he said, raising an ironic eyebrow.

"Yes, but why?"

"Insomnia has bought it."

"Pull the other. What's really going on?"

"The restaurant is closed," he said. "The deal's done and dusted. Get over it. Move on."

She had reeled from the café into Grafton Street. She couldn't believe it. Closing Bewley's was on a par with closing the Ritz in London. Unthinkable!

And that little gurrier telling her to get over it, to move on!

But the outcry had been loud and long and the coffee house had been saved. For a while Bewley's had lost its way a little, but now it was back to normal — certainly more expensive — but still here with its high ceiling, stained-glass windows, crystal chandeliers, giant palms, wonderful coffee: its lineage intact.

*

It would be fitting to continue reading *Ulysses* in a place that its author doubtless frequented: maybe he had sat on this very seat. She dived under the table and surfaced clutching the book.

Get a grip, she thought. Thousands of idiots like you come to Dublin every year to read the damn thing, to follow in the footsteps of a fictional character and to ...

"You're about four months too late or eight months too early," said a tiny man, sitting at the far end of the booth opposite a tall elderly gent.

Niamh did not bother to reply to what she supposed was a drunken outburst. She opened the book at where she had placed a bookmark months before. Page 172. But she couldn't make head or tail of the disjointed sentences, couldn't remember any of the characters mentioned, hadn't a clue how the plot had developed up to that point.

I'll have to start over again. I'll start and finish the book while I'm here. It will be a beginning and a closure of sorts.

Although I'm not sure that is in keeping with my particular circumstances.

So that's no good.

She pondered for a moment.

Ah, feck it! she thought, I'll just read it.

She turned to the last page to check the number of pages; jotted 912 on her napkin; subtracted the 140 pages of the introduction and divided 772 by 6. If she concentrated on the novel she would have to read 128.6 (recurring) pages per day to complete within the timeframe available. If she read the entire book — she divided 912 by 6 — that would be 152 pages each day.

A piece of Bewley's cake!

*

She took a right turn out of the restaurant and headed for The Green.

The sun skimmed the treetops, peeped through shrubs, gilded pathways with a blinding light. She would skirt the lake and then head for the fountains. She would find a seat and begin reading *Ulysses*.

The park was crowded. The unseasonably warm weather had brought people out in droves. Workers of every nationality lounged on the grass, eating and drinking. Many more strolled along, enjoying the fine autumn weather and a brief respite from the hustle and bustle of the city; toddlers fed the ducks and swans.

"A Dublin accent is as rare as a devout Catholic in this city," one of her brothers had told her a few years previously. "The place is crawling with foreigners and we're too small a city to accommodate them all."

"The place was always crawling with foreigners," Niamh had laughed, "but we used to call them culchies."

"You can laugh all you want, but I'm tellin' you, if this continues there'll be skin and hair flying, make no mistake."

She had dismissed his fears as alarmist twaddle. The Irish were famous for their hospitality and Joyce himself had testified to their gentleness, but on more recent visits she had been regaled with stories of the problems attendant on a sudden and dramatic increase in population. Quiet residential areas were being disrupted as properties were filled to bursting with newly arrived immigrants. Noise and litter increased: health and education services were under severe strain and tensions grew apace.

A few months previously, during a visit to London, Niamh had heard the President of Ireland tell her story of contemporary Ireland. The President was delighted that many thousands of Irish emigrants were returning home for good and that they were being joined by people from all over the world. This twenty-first century Diaspora was leading to the enrichment of Irish culture, she claimed, and all was hunky-dory.

Of the two versions of the state of the nation Niamh preferred the President's. However, when she ran it past her brother, during a telephone conversation a few days after her London visit, his response was not encouraging.

"That one says more than her prayers," he said. "It's all right for her. It's easy to be upbeat when you live in a mansion far away from the noise and filth. If she's so delighted she could invite a few hundred of them to join her in *Aras an Uchterain* and, while she's at it, she could start a building programme in the park to accommodate the native Irish who can't afford homes."

Niamh paused on the tiddler O'Connell Bridge to gaze at the expanse of lake to the east, and then moved on to the centre of the park. Circular beds of scarlet geraniums and pink dahlias splashed the scene with vivid colour, but all the benches were occupied so she kept walking.

She stopped to look at the statues of The Three Fates engrossed in their endless cycle of spinning, measuring and cutting.

"Do you see tha'? Do you see tha'?" A man stood, hands in pockets, his head nodding vigorously towards the statues.

"I'd want to be blind not to," Niamh replied. "It's a pretty big sculpture."

"Not tha'," he said, "tha'," nodding more vigorously still. At Niamh's look of bemusement he added, "The plaque, the plaque."

"What about it?"

"It says that the monument was presented in 1997, but that's a feckin' lie, so it is. The German people gave it to the Irish in 1956 for looking after refugee kids after the Second World War, so they did, and some eejit in Dublin Corporation go' it wrong." He turned away and walked towards Leeson Street gate.

They should never have reduced the intake of The Gorman, Niamh thought.

As she headed in a northerly direction a young couple emerged from the dense shrubs near the memorial. The young man picked leaves from the woman's hair, brushed his hand lovingly across her back to dislodge bits of twigs. The woman kissed him tenderly on the lips.

Niamh had been walking for some time without noticing where she was going. Unwittingly, she had retraced her steps to the main entrance of the park. Directly opposite was a structure that made her shudder every time she saw it. The glass and white metal of this tasteless confection ruined the symmetry of the square, was completely out of place. The gaudy edifice winked brazenly in the sun and she turned away in disgust. The elaborate design was intended to cloak the true function of the building (yet another shopping mall), to suggest a giant conservatory, which would, apparently, provide an imaginative link with the park. As far as she was concerned it resembled a monstrous wedding-cake that would, over time, metamorphose into a great rusting hulk.

And another thing, when she'd turned her back one winter, the nearby Green Cinema, a wonderful example of art deco design, where she had experienced the magic of her first grown-up kiss, had been demolished.

*

What to do? She had spent the half hour since entering The Green through Fusilier's Arch, (erected in 1907 to commemorate Irish soldiers who had died in the Second Boer War) wandering aimlessly when her intention had been to soak up the atmosphere, to sit and watch the world go by, to begin her re-reading of *Ulysses*. She checked her watch. It was quarter-past one. There was still plenty of time to carry out her original plan. Back through the archway (or Traitor's Gate as it had been known locally), follow the path by the lake and then …

"Excuse me, ma'am, is this St. Stephen's Green Park?"

Niamh hesitated for a moment thinking to ignore the enquiry and let someone else deal with yet another Yank looking for his roots.

"Hello, there, ma'am. It's me," the voice said, "from the bus."

She looked skywards and into the friendly eyes of the young man she'd met earlier that day. "Yes, you're in the right place," she said and walked on.

"Could I ask you a question, ma'am?" his voice followed her. She kept going. "Excuse me, could I ask you a question?" he said more loudly. She stopped and turned to face him.

"What do you want to know?"

"I'm looking for Yeats' Garden. The book says it's in this park, but no one seems to know where it is. I've asked and asked but most folk don't seem to speak English. I guess I need a native Dubliner."

"I wouldn't count on them knowing either," Niamh said, "I'm not sure anyone in this city is interested in a poet who's been dead for over seventy years."

"But he was a Nobel Laureate, ma'am, and Dublin is a city with a fine literary tradition."

"I bet you ten-to-one if we find a genuine jackeen under thirty in this park they won't have a clue where Yeats' Garden is."

"You're on."

Twenty minutes and twelve enquiries later they agreed to call a halt. Five of the people they'd stopped claimed to be Dubliners, born and bred, but none had heard of Yeats. One young man, hoping for a prize, chanced his arm.

"Yeah, of course I've heard of Yeats," he said, "me ma knew him. He sang with a show-band, so he did."

Niamh led the young American towards the steps that appeared to lead nowhere and into the paved memorial garden that was graced by a Henry Moore sculpture. She sat on a stone ledge for a while as he wandered around the small space, photographing it from every angle.

"They're for my grandma," he said, aware that he was being watched. "She's a fan of Yeats. I was named after him," he said with a hint of embarrassment. "My given names are William Butler, though everyone calls me W.B. My grandma read about this memorial on the Internet so she asked me to come see."

"You're a good lad," she said, rising stiffly, "enjoy the rest of your stay."

She had reached the exit when she heard his call. "Hey, ma'am, you didn't collect your winnings, ten-to-one, remember?"

In the end she agreed that lunch at the Shelbourne would more than pay off his debt, provided he stopped calling her ma'am.

*

At half-past three she sent him on his way with a list of her favourite places.

"If you had just one afternoon in Dublin," he had asked, "what would you do?"

"I'd leave the city," she said. "I'd take the DART to Killiney and walk back along the beach towards Dalkey. I'd go to Bulloch Harbour and watch the fishing boats; I'd go to Sandycove and visit the Martello Tower where Stephen Dedalus stayed."

"Stephen Dedalus was a fictional character," he said with a grin, "he couldn't have stayed anywhere."

"We haven't time to discuss the nature of fiction, but if you want my advice on what to see, just listen."

"Sure thing, Aunty Niamh."

*

She stood on the path outside the hotel and watched him walk away from her towards Grafton Street. On his way to Connolly Station to catch the train he would pop into Bewley's, perhaps have a cup of coffee, just so he could tell his grandma he'd been there; he would nip into Trinity College to see the Book of Kells. Niamh had suggested a circular route from there: along Dame Street, a right into Temple Bar (every youngster had to visit The Bar), across Ha'penny Bridge, a quick dart into The Winding Stair Book Shop to browse through the books, back towards O'Connell Bridge and anyone would tell him how to find the station.

She watched until he disappeared from view and then crossed the road and entered the park through the granite monoliths of Tonehenge.

The large space was strangely quiet. It was late afternoon and only a few stragglers remained; mothers no longer lingered at the lake encouraging their young to throw bread at, possibly, the best-fed ducks in the world. The workers who had lounged in the sun at lunchtime had gone. With the exception of those who used the park as a pleasant thoroughfare from one side of the square to the other the only noticeable presence was a group of men and women who had claimed the bandstand as their living quarters and were sharing the contents of a bottle and a couple of cans.

Niamh welcomed the peace and quiet. Her meeting with W.B. had unsettled her. Unwittingly, he had scratched at emotions that were, despite the passing of long years, raw and tender: emotions she was determined to confront. She had wanted to approach these feelings slowly, to sneak up on them, to edge closer, like a cat hunting its prey, but W.B. with his endless questions, his guileless enthusiasm, had pushed her too soon.

In an attempt to restore her equilibrium she returned to the park and strolled slowly around its winding pathways.

She had been reading *Ulysses* for over an hour and still hadn't dented the surface of the introduction.

She had made a mistake.

She should have grasped the nettle.

Should have gone straight to the novel.

Instead, she'd spent her precious time going round and round in circles trying to follow the ramblings of some academic who waffled with great authority about the significance of history memory mythology gender the manipulation of language and form plus another thousand and one aspects of the literary that made this novel not a novel made this work of fiction more than a work of fiction made this literary genius more than a literary genius.

The memory of her previous difficulties with the book came flooding back. She threw it from her in disgust. She should never have brought it with her on this trip: the dreaded demons were enough to deal with.

For some time past she thought she might be heading for a breakdown, losing the bit she had. She'd been waking in the night, overwhelmed by a sense of great tragedy, great sadness, a terrifying loss. She would lie, crying into the dark, pleading not to be left alone. But she had no idea with whom she was pleading, no idea why, so late in life, she was suddenly afflicted in this way. In her waking hours she couldn't remember an event of sufficient magnitude to explain the nightly terrors, couldn't imagine what the loss might be. And she could find no name for the whirlpool of sensation that engulfed her. 'Nightmare' didn't seem to fit the bill. 'Nightmare', she thought, would involve place, people, sounds, smells; but none of these figured. She was aware only of a huge vacuum, a swirling nothingness.

The sense of loss was so pervasive, so all-consuming, that she was convinced she must have had a twin she had never known, from whom she had been separated at birth (she was obviously watching too many back-to-your-roots television programmes). She had gone as far as checking the records of births for the year she was born, but could find no evidence to support her theory.

After much agonizing she had decided the only way to tackle the problem was to return to her beginnings. She would visit the scenes of her childhood in the hope that they might offer some clue as to what was happening to her. She realized that this was a high-risk strategy, that she might recall an incident so terrible that she had buried it without trace. And what, at her age, would she do with this unpalatable knowledge? She was unable to find a satisfactory answer to this question so almost gave up on her proposed trip. But another question raised its head. Could she continue to endure waking in the night, crying into the darkness for someone to come and assuage her terrible loneliness? This was a question she could answer. And the answer was no.

She picked up the book and hugged it to her chest as she would a baby. She had brought Joyce's novel with her, she realized, not simply to distract her or because she was determined to finish reading it, but because some instinct told her that within the tangled coherence of its plot and the concise verbosity of its language might lie the key to her turmoil. If, as she had been given to understand, all human life was in this work, then surely her story must be there somewhere.

Waiting to be discovered.

*

She rose from the bed and went to the lavatory. After she'd relieved herself and washed her hands, taking care not to glance in the mirror, she returned to the bedroom and sank onto the bed.

It was seven o'clock and she was hungry, but she didn't feel like facing the bustle of the dining room alone, nor did she want to pay the exorbitant prices the hotel charged for room service.

She turned on the television news and promptly turned it off again. The world was in freefall: it was enough to make you want to expire on the spot.

The phone rang, making her leap a good foot off the bed. Her left hand flew to her heart while she reached for the receiver with her right. She waited a moment and took deep breaths. As she lifted the phone a great guffaw of laughter sprang from her mouth.

"Aunty Niamh, are you all right?"

By now helpless with laughter, she fell back onto the bed, clutching her stomach.

"Aunty Niamh, ma'am, are you okay? Can I call someone? Are you …"

With a supreme effort she pulled herself together. "I'm fine, I'm ..." She was off again, laughing until the tears streamed down her face. "I was thinking," she said and broke down once again. "The phone made me jump," she said, "and I was thinking ... I was thinking that that was the best jump I'd had in a bed for many years."

"You're a game old bird, Aunty Niamh. My grandma would surely like you."

"I'll have less of the old from you young W.B."

*

"So, you're a Joycean as well as a fan of Yeats."

"Sure, I like Joyce, who wouldn't? The man was a genius."

"Do you think all geniuses are, by virtue of their genius, likeable?"

"No, ma'am, I don't, but they are to be admired."

When she had managed to control her hysteria W.B. had invited her to dinner. In following the itinerary she had devised he had spotted her hotel as he chugged past on the DART. On his return journey he had disembarked at Booterstown Station and called her from reception.

At first she had baulked at the idea. A young man with only one night in Dublin should be out there where it's at, where it's happening, letting it all hang out, where it's wicked, shaking his stuff ...

"I'm leaving first thing in the morning," he said, "so I need an early night. It would be great to have dinner with a genuine Dubliner so if you would do me the honour I'll head on back to the hotel at about ten o'clock."

She opened her mouth to argue further, thought of his earnest blue eyes set in a handsome tanned face. Ah, feck it, she thought, I may be beyond touching, but I can still admire the view. She did however insist that dinner was her treat.

She had ordered her favourite — pan-fried salmon bass — caught on a flooding tide at Rosslare Strand the night before, according to the waiter: no sauce required, just the succulent white flesh crumbling with freshness. She chose asparagus and boiled potatoes, liberally coated with Irish butter, to accompany her fish.

W.B. resisted her urgings to order the same and opted for a bowl of steaming coddle. Niamh pointed out that coddle had been the staple food of the Dublin poor — a stew that accommodated any and all sorts of scraps — bits of bacon and sausage, potato, onion, peas and anything else that could be found to bulk it out for large ravenous families, but he was undeterred.

She chose a crisp Pinot Grigio, a perfect complement to the delicate taste of her fish. Although she suggested that Guinness might not be the ideal accompaniment for coddle, he ordered it anyway. "When in Ireland ..." he said, with a shrug of his broad shoulders. On reflection she thought he might have a point. No doubt Guinness had been the tipple of choice for the Dublin slum-dwellers who had invented the dish in the first place.

"So how much of Joyce have you read?" she asked before sipping her wine.

"Just about everything, ma'am."

"Everything!"

"Yes, ma'am."
"Including *Finnegans Wake*?"
"Sure thing."
"How old are you?"
"Twenty-five, ma'am."
"Don't tell me. You started at seven years old and have learnt his entire opus by heart."
"No, ma'am, I chose Joyce as an option at university and was hooked from the word go."

*

"Do you believe androgyny is the state to which all men should aspire?" she asked, remembering some such claim made in the introduction she'd struggled with a few hours previously.

"Run that by me again." He raised his eyebrows as he looked at her over the rim of his glass.

"I wondered if you agreed with Joyce that man's salvation lies in his willingness to embrace his feminine side."

"I don't recall Joyce making that claim, ma'am."

"But surely that's what lies at the very heart of his characterization of Bloom?" Niamh treated W.B. to a quizzical smile.

"My guess is that in Bloom Joyce wanted to show how a man can be unsexed if he cannot control his wife." W.B. said.

"What an interesting reading of the text." Niamh raised her glass. "*Sláinte!*" she said.

*

She slept fitfully. The long day, the strange bed, the roar of the traffic, the unaccustomed wine were, she knew, contributory factors. But these were not the only causes of her unrest.

The highpoint of her evening with W.B turned out to be the exchange about Joyce. After that, despite her best efforts to deflect him, his conversation returned again and again to his grandmother. At first she thought this was because he saw his much-loved relative as her contemporary, someone who had grown up in Ireland at about the same time, a point of contact for his elderly dinner companion. But as the evening wore on she realized it was more than that. There was an obsessive quality to the way he returned, again and again, to the topic of his grandmother.

If he picked at a scab as compulsively as he talks about her, Niamh thought, the wound would never heal. There was she thinking a young man wanted to spend an evening with her for the joy of her wit and intelligence when all he wanted was a surrogate granny.

"If your grandmother came from Dublin why are you haring off to Cork tomorrow?" she asked.

"Grandpa's folks came from Cork," he said, "so grandma asked me to go see if I can locate the family house or even the family grave. She met my grandpa in the States so she never saw his home town."

Niamh took a generous swig of wine. "I'm surprised your grandmother didn't come with you. It would have been a great opportunity for her to see all these places first hand."

"We'd planned for years to make the trip together," he said, and tears started in his eyes. "When I was a little boy she made up a rhyme.
                  You and me, W.B.
                  You and me.

> We'll cross the sea, W.B.
> We'll cross the sea.
> To see all there is to see,
> In Ireland.

But we left it too late. Grandma is … she's …" he wiped the back of his hand across his eyes, "she's too sick to travel," he said.

Niamh signalled to the waiter. "Another glass of wine please. Make it a large one."

"You're lucky," W.B. had said to her as they parted.

"How'sss that?" Niamh was aware that she was slurring her words.

"You've made the trip while there's still time. You haven't left it till it's too late."

Portobello Barracks, where Niamh was born and raised, had been built by the British in 1810 and had expanded throughout the nineteenth century to house soldiers and their families. When, in 1922, the British finally left the twenty-six counties of the Irish Free State, the Irish Army moved in.

The compound was divided into two distinct sections — the military quarters where the administrative arm of the service, the chaplaincy, billets for single soldiers, the stables, the armoury and officers' housing were situated. Alongside, separated by green railings and a gate manned by a military policeman, was the married quarters for non-commissioned officers and privates.

The married quarters comprised seven separate blocks of flats, each with two storeys and were identified by the letters of the alphabet, from A to G. Most of the flats had one or two bedrooms, with the occasional, much-coveted, three-bedroom accommodation. A large field bounded the compound to the west. In theory this open space was used for military manoeuvres: in practice it was an unofficial playground for the soldiers' children. The children did not confine themselves to the field, however. They used the entire compound of the married quarters to play out their fantasies.

*

"We will fight and die for freedom,
To the shores of Tripoli.
To the shores of Tripoli.
To the shores of Tripoli.
We will fight and die for freedom,
To the shores of Tripoli."

"Halt!" Rabba' O'Hare brought his young warriors (including Niamh's brother Paul) to a standstill in the space between blocks A and B of Portobello Barracks.

The young commander and his infant soldiers sang lustily, replacing the word 'freedom' with the word I-r-e-land, unaware that it had been unnecessary for anyone to fight and die for Ireland all the way to North Africa, but historical veracity was not their main concern. They knew nothing of the First Barbary War, fought in 1805 by The United States of America against Morocco, Algiers, Tunis and Tripoli in defence of their ships which were regularly attacked by pirates; the tiny soldiers were also unaware that the song they sang so lustily, paid tribute to a daring raid carried out by American marines during that war.

Rabba' and his band had been introduced to the song during a visit to The Prinner, (The Princess) the local picture house. Having enjoyed their weekly episode of *Flash Gordon*, the current follier-upper, they sat through the main feature, *To The Shores of Tripoli*, shot in glorious Technicolor and starring the Irish beauty, Maureen O'Hara. They watched, enthralled, as the fearless warriors of America marched with heads held high, singing The Marines' Hymn.

Rabba' and company's skinny chests had swelled with valour and at the first opportunity they applied the sentiment of the song to their own particular circumstances. Niamh's father might rage at the "pernicious propaganda promulgated through American and British films", but the lads of the barracks devoured it with relish and relived their cinematic experience in their play.

*

At the precise moment that Rabba's platoon snapped to a halt a rotund boy tentatively rounded the corner of B Block. The miniature soldiers spotted the youngster and immediately the stirring march changed to a jig.

> "You have a fat arse,
> You're a great tub of lard.
> You have a fat arse,
> You're a great tub of lard.
> You have a fat arse,
> You're a great tub of laaaard,
> And your farts are louder than thunder."

"At eashe!" Rabba' O'Hare shouted. "At eashe!" he lisped again as spittle whistled through the wide gap where his buckteeth had, until recently, grown.

The absence of these teeth offered a reprieve from the sort of jeering and slagging meted out to the hapless lad who had tried to pass unnoticed. Rabba' was grateful to nature for having removed the ugly protuberances. He said ten Hail Marys every night in the hope that Jesus' mother would ensure that his new teeth grew small and straight. He harboured a secret wish that when the miracle occurred, instead of Rabba', people would call him by his given name, Aloysius; then no one would make fun of him ever again.

Attempting to regain control of the situation, Rabba', aka Aloysius, once more shouted, "At eashe". His troops looked uncertainly from one to another and back to their gummy commander. He removed his hurley stick from his shoulder and placed it, curved side to the ground, along the outside of his left leg. His most loyal soldiers followed suit, but the remainder couldn't resist the temptation presented by Bum D'Arcy who was running for his life towards A Block.

*

Niamh and Bum's young sister Marie looked on in mute fascination as the boys sped past, shouting and hollering, baying for blood. Although Patrick D'Arcy's nickname was cruel, it had a certain integrity. There was no denying that it was based on an incontrovertible truth: Patrick's bum was the fattest part of his fat young body.

Patrick ran with a speed that gave lie to the notion that obese people are slower than their slimmer counterparts, but it was a speed born of desperation and he couldn't keep it up. By the time he reached the stairs that ran along the side of A Block and which would lead him to the sanctuary of his home, his stubby little legs were buckling beneath him. He had made the third step when a hand grabbed for his ankle and caught it. He pulled with all his might, but others joined the first assailant and they jumped on him with savage glee, punching and kicking, all the while chanting their cruel ditty,

> "You have a fat arse,
> You're a great tub of lard.
> You have a fat arse,

You're a great tub of lard."

"Stop that now. Do ye hear me? I said, stop that now. Leave that lad alone. Ye're a gang of little *scuts*. I'll tell yer mammies on every one of ye." Niamh's mother's voice rang out loud and furious and the flaying arms and legs became quiet and still. "Go on," she said, her voice still trembling with anger, "go on, or so help me god, I'll swing for the lot of ye."

Patrick didn't stop to thank his saviour. Red-faced and ashamed, he limped and hopped up the stairs.

*

The D'Arcys were different from the other families who lived in blocks A and B of Portobello Barracks: they were, every last one of them, fatter than their neighbours, but they were also kinder, more hospitable and more gentle — characteristics that the people of catholic Ireland were taught to value because of their Christ-like qualities. Unfortunately for the D'Arcys only a handful of the barracks' residents were up to the challenge of their religion: the actions of the remainder fell well short of their christian aspirations and they treated their kindly neighbours with derision and, occasionally, unthinking cruelty.

*

Niamh and Marie had become friends because they were both outcasts of a sort: Marie was fat and Niamh was a carrot-top. Their friendship, initially based on expediency, quickly became close and warm. Every morning during the school holidays, at nine o'clock sharp, Marie knocked on the door of number one A Block.

"Come in Marie," Niamh's mother shouted, without bothering to check who was there. "She'll be with you in a minute. I'm just plaiting her hair."

Niamh never made the journey upwards to where her friend lived. Green iron railings enclosed the veranda along the upper floor and the gap between the vertical rods was, she thought, just big enough for her skinny frame to slip through if someone had a mind to give her a sneaky shove. Despite her mother's assurances that she was in no danger, she refused to venture. She had witnessed unprovoked attacks on the helpless too often to be convinced that she was entirely safe.

*

Niamh and Marie spent their days together out front in the wide gravelled space between A and B Blocks, skipping, playing ball games or piggy-beds. As the day wore on and they were crowded out by dozens of more boisterous children, they retired to the grassy patch behind the flats and did the buttercup test to see who liked butter best, made daisy chains and, if they were sure no-one could see, played mammies and daddies.

They had just one falling out during their short friendship; it had been Niamh's fault and she still cringed with shame when she remembered how it came about.

They were sitting in the sun, making daisy chains, when Bernie Mulligan appeared. She stood for several minutes looking at them and then sidled along the wall of the flats.

"Why do you play with her?" she asked.

They both looked up in surprise, but didn't answer.

"I said why do you play with fa' face?"

There was no doubting who the question was aimed at. Niamh looked quickly at her friend. Marie's sunny smile had disappeared and her round face was puckered in alarm. She met Niamh's eyes and then looked down to where the unfinished daisy chain lay in her lap.

"At least she's not stupid like you."

The kick came low and swift and caught Niamh a glancing blow on the side of the head. "Who do you think you're calling stupa'?" Bernie shouted. "You and fa'y are well met."

They sat dazed and numb for a few moments and then rose in silence, the withering daisies falling from their laps. They walked towards the side of the block. Still mute with shock, Marie climbed the stairs and Niamh walked around the corner to her home.

The falling out came next day.

Marie arrived at nine o'clock and they went out to play but unable to muster enthusiasm for their usual games they sat, forlornly, at the edge of the path outside Niamh's front door.

"Why did you let her get away with it?" Niamh asked. Marie said nothing, but she started to cry. Triumphantly, Niamh kept on. "It was your fault that she kicked me and you didn't do anything. You're a fat coward."

Marie's bowed head shot up and she grabbed hold of Niamh's golden-red plait. "Take that back," she said.

"I will not, you are a coward and you are fat." Niamh's hand lashed out and, as though to prove her point, she caught hold of her friend's ample cheek and twisted the soft flesh.

"Niamh O'Riordan, get in the house this minute." Niamh's grip slackened at the sound of her mother's voice. Seizing her opportunity Marie rose and ran towards the stairs.

For the remaining week of the school holidays Niamh waited for the nine o'clock knock on the door, but it didn't come. "Go upstairs and call for her," her mother said. "Tell her you're sorry."

"But she pulled my hair first," was Niamh's rejoinder each time.

"She's your best friend, it doesn't matter who says sorry. Just do it."

By the time she'd accepted the wisdom of her mother's words it was too late to make amends.

She looked upwards at the Spire, straining her neck, back and back until she almost keeled over. She was in the middle of O'Connell Street, standing next to the monument that occupied the space left by Nelson's Pillar. There had been many attempts to rid the capital of The Pillar during its one hundred and fifty two year tenure. All had failed until former members of the IRA took matters into their own hands and blew it up early one March morning in 1966.

It would be true to say that The Monument of Light, to give the Spire its official name, had not received the whole-hearted approval of Dubliners: many thought the 398 foot stainless steel pin aesthetically uninteresting; others thought it a waste of money that could have been put to better use. Ignoring the pretensions of the planners, jackeens had named the twenty-first century monument 'The Stiletto in the Ghetto' or, more mundanely, 'The Spike'.

*

Despite her heavy evening with W.B. she had set the alarm for six o'clock, determined that her literary journey should unfold alongside her ramblings around Dublin.

She had abandoned the introduction to *Ulysses* and had followed Stephen from the moment of his waking to his meanderings along Sandymount Strand. She had noted the random manner in which Joyce introduced details of the story and the characters; had thought that perhaps the old milk woman symbolized a decaying Ireland. She had sympathy with Stephen's irritation with Buck Mulligan — that great big lump would get on anyone's nerves. She knew that there were layers of meaning that escaped her, but she was pleased with her progress. She had hopped out of bed, showered, ate a full Irish breakfast, caught the number seven bus and here she was, ready for the off.

She walked down Henry Street. Arnott's was still there but, alas, Woollies' and Roche's Stores had gone. She took a right into Moore Street, which had retained much of its old character: dozens of stalls ran along both sides of the street and the air was heavy with the sweet and earthy smell of fruit and vegetables. The vendors' voices rang out, urging shoppers to buy "delicious apples, oranges and bananas, fresh today, the best and cheapest produce in Dublin."

"How can they be fresh today," a man asked, picking up an apple, "when they're all squashed and brown?"

"Keep your hands off the produce, don't touch the fru'", the vendor cried, ignoring his question. "You can ea' me, but you can't squeeze me, as the bishop said to the reverend mother."

Niamh wandered on down the street, taking care not to lose her footing on the slippery cobblestones. She had always hated this noisy smelly place — its stalls and old prams overflowing with over-ripe produce: was repulsed by its overblown women who peppered their urgings to buy with vulgarities. The cacophonous mixture of trundling barrows, the roar of the hawkers, kids squealing and screaming in delight as they ran madly between stalls, customers laughing and shouting, trying to make themselves heard, was too much for her. The assault on her senses flattened her, made her feel exhausted, filled her with a desperate desire to escape, to run away and find a quiet place.

But her attitude had changed shortly before her father died. A native of Wexford, he had spent his adult life in the capital city and, like most country people, his defence against the slick spivvy ways of the jackeens was to disparage them and their customs, to cling fiercely to his own kind and his own ways of doing. For him Moore Street epitomized everything he hated about Dublin: it was loud, brash, vulgar and — the greatest sin of all for a man who caught fish fresh from the sea and grew his own vegetables — its produce was frequently on the turn.

But late in life, when he had been retired from the army for many years and had in his possession a free bus pass, he had taken to travelling into the city centre and returning with bags bulging with purchases from the Moore Street vendors.

"Stinking rubbish," her mother would say, when he presented her with his booty, "That lot see you coming."

"I'm going into town. Do you want to come?" her father had asked when she was home for a brief visit.

"Okay," she had answered. "Yeah, you're on."

When they disembarked at The Pillar he headed straight for Moore Street.

"Hello, there, darlin' how are ya? I didn't think you were coming to-day, I thought you were going to stand me up." The stallholder's face was wreathed in smiles. "What do ya fancy? I've got huge melons, if ya'd like a couple, but no squeezing, do ya hear?"

Niamh moved away, but she kept an eye on him from a distance. Her father continued from stall to stall, returning the banter, his eyes twinkling: his face alight with a spark and energy she hadn't witnessed for years.

Since his death she always visited Moore Street when in Dublin. Amongst its noise and smells the presence of the frail but indomitable spirit of her father's elderly self was more palpable than anywhere else.

As she surveyed the street she realized that Moore Street Market might offer a blueprint for the future. Although the stalls were, as far as she could tell, still owned by native vendors, a few Asian and African traders occupied the small shops on either side of the street. If newcomers had made inroads here and lived to tell the tale then it was possible that immigrants could integrate elsewhere.

Trade could be the saviour of modern Ireland.

Perhaps the end of the line for the saints and scholars had finally arrived.

*

Back to Henry Street, towards Mary Street. Someone had told her that Joyce, as one of a consortium of small businessmen, had opened The Volta, the first Irish cinema, in this street in 1909.

There you are.

The great man himself had been involved in commerce.

Along Mary Street, remembering the Dolls' Hospital, long gone, where her china doll had been mended when her brothers jumped out of hiding, giving her the fright of her life and causing her to drop it and smash it into a dozen pieces. She had bawled for an hour, howled and sobbed, only stopped when her brothers had been strapped and sent to bed without tea.

Left into Upper Liffey Street and she was almost at the Ha'penny Bridge. Past Hector Grey's where once you could buy toys galore, a penny a go, now closed and dilapidated with half the letters missing from the name and the shutters splattered with graffiti. The Woollen Mills were still on the opposite side of the street and although she never in her life bought a thing in that place she couldn't resist popping in.

It was an institution.

All the bales of heavy woollen cloth had gone. The place was bursting at the seams with zips, buttons and frippery, with the occasional Aran sweater and kilt: upstairs, reams and reams of vivid silks, satins and chiffons and a man from the sub-continent chatting on his mobile phone.

Time for a break.

Up the rickety stairs of The Winding Stair.

She pushed the door open.

Instead of tables covered in red and white gingham and a variety of ill-matched wooden chairs occupied by students and cool dudes and framed by wall to ceiling shelves of second-hand books, she was confronted by a café decorated in the minimalist style favoured by the makeover artists who popped up on television every night of the week.

"We're closed," the young woman who was wiping the counter yelled.

"What's happened?" Niamh asked.

"What d' you mean what's happened?"

"Where has everything gone? What have they done with all the books?"

"We've had a makeover, we use the books to accessorize," she said, pointing to a slim bookcase.

"But why are you not open for coffee?"

"There's a notice downstairs which clearly states that we open for lunch at midday."

Niamh stumbled down the stairs and onto the quays. She walked over Ha'penny Bridge without noticing where she was. She kept going until she arrived in George's Street and made for the Arcade. She ordered a cappuccino and Danish and attacked them with gusto.

They had turned one of her favourite cafés, where she'd spent many hours reading and gazing at the Liffey, into a jakes.

She took her book from her bag. Maybe if she read for a while it would help her deal with the shock.

"I've read tha'."

Niamh ignored the woman sitting next to her at the long communal table.

"I've read tha'. It's grea'."

"I've just started."

"Oh, you'll really enjoy it; it's leppin'."

"Good."

"Yeah, there's this fella, Stephen. He's a bit of an upstart, thinks he's better than everyone else; thinks he's so clever. I hate people like tha', so I do". She took a great gulp of tea and continued. "Have you go' to the part where he meets Leopold?"

"No, like I said, I've only just begun."

"Ah, Leopold is grea', a lovely man. I love Leopold so I do. He's every woman's dream man. A proper gentleman, so he is. I think all Jewish men are like tha'."

*

She was out on the street again. If she took a left she would be heading for Aungier Street and maintaining the integrity of her circular route.

Possibly.

It depended on how circular a circular route should be.

Anyhow keep going.

Along George's Street.

A quick glance to the right confirmed that Cassidy's had indeed vanished. But she knew that — it had been gone for years. Although as a child she'd never been inside the premier shop for girls' clothes, it had exerted a great deal of power over her young life. She knew of its existence because of Margaret O'Brien.

Margaret O'Brien was the prettiest girl in infants. Her perfect, golden ringlets compressed and expanded like rows of precision springs as she walked around the playground, invariably holding the hand of the most coveted boy in the class. Niamh and the other girls hated her, not simply because she was pretty, nor because her bows were always starched and upright, nor because David Findlater loved her, but mostly because she boasted, loudly, that all her clothes were bought from Cassidy's.

Niamh remembered a rare occasion when she had been taken into town by her mother and found herself outside the bewitching shop. As she realized where she was she ground to a halt by the large plate-glass window and stared longingly at the display of colourful coats, dresses, skirts and jumpers. She willed her mother to say, "That turquoise dress — the one with the white smocking and large bow would look only gorgeous on you Niamh, we'll buy it for you because you've been a good girl." Instead her mother pulled impatiently at Niamh's hand and dragged her away. At that moment Niamh's hatred of Margaret was like that of a cat for a dog — snarling and savage.

Luckily, Margaret's dad died soon after.

And she left the school for good.

The flats in married quarters were primitive — they had no bathrooms and, until the late 1950s, some families had to make do with outside lavatories, but they were an attractive option for hard-pressed residents who paid a nominal rent and very little for the coal, logs and turf delivered weekly, thus offering a degree of financial security for families who, because of their adherence to catholic teaching, found it difficult to control their numbers.

For the men, the advantages of living in married quarters were social as well as financial: the adjacent military quarters housed the mess for both corporals and sergeants where drink was cheap, and many hours could be spent away from the noise and turmoil of family life, playing billiards and cards.

It was military policy to pay a percentage of soldiers' wages directly to their wives. Without this arrangement the grim struggle for survival would, for many women, have been grimmer still.

During the late 1930s, Dublin Corporation started a building programme intended, primarily, to re-house slum-dwellers from the city centre, but soldiers and their families were also eligible to apply for one of these properties.

Many army wives harried their husbands to apply for their dream homes. The withdrawal of conjugal rights was threatened, but it was an empty threat, as catholic women were required to protect their husbands from occasions of sin by supplying sex on demand. The men who allowed themselves to be convinced of the wisdom of moving from married quarters tended to be men who preferred the company of their families to that of their military cronies: men who were moderate drinkers, who didn't fit easily into the macho culture of army life.

*

As Niamh set off for school at the start of September 1950, still estranged from her best friend, she was unaware that the culture of the barracks, aided and abetted by Dublin Corporation's housing policy, was about to inflict a cruel blow.

Niamh and Marie attended different schools. Each morning Marie left home at 8.20a.m. and made her way to St. Clare's School in Harold's Cross. Ten minutes later Niamh started out for St. Louis's National School in Rathmines.

For the first four mornings of term Niamh peered longingly through net curtains as the podgy figure of her best friend waddled by. On the fifth day she saw Marie hesitate outside the front door. Not wishing to be caught in the act, Niamh jumped quickly back into the room and tripped over her younger brother. By the time she had returned to the window Marie had gone.

Niamh spent the day at school in a state of extreme agitation that earned her a telling-off from Sister Scholastica. But she didn't care. She had made a decision. After school she would climb the stairs at the side of A Block. She would walk along the veranda (keeping well away from the railings) and she would call for her estranged friend.

At the sound of the four o'clock bell, like a greyhound from a trap, she leapt from her desk and ran all the way home. She threw her school bag onto the front door mat and hurried around the corner.

A large van was parked close to the path. Corporal D'Arcy and Marie's uncle were struggling with a chest of drawers and Mrs. D'Arcy came close behind, clutching a bulging bag.

"Hello there Ginger," Corporal D'Arcy called, "You've still got a liking for those carrots I see."

"I'm going to call for Marie," Niamh said.

"Marie's not there, dear," Mrs. D'Arcy smiled and her eyes disappeared into folds of pink flesh.

"When will she be home?"

"She's not coming home *a leanbh*. We're moving to a new house and her Aunt Bridget picked her and Patrick up from school. They've gone ahead."

"But when will she be back?"

"She's not coming back *a stór*. We're going for good." Mrs. D'Arcy voice tinkled with pleasure.

Niamh stood rooted to the spot, trying to understand the enormity of what had been said. "But when will I see her?" she asked in a hushed tone as though talking to herself.

"When we've settled in you can come and visit," Mrs. D'Arcy said, before disappearing into the back of the van.

Niamh watched as Mr. D'Arcy and his brother climbed aboard; she stood still as the engine spluttered and roared; she turned and watched the van's slow progress as it trundled off towards the Cross Gate. Children followed, shouting and hollering. Seamus Deane tried to *scut* the van by grabbing hold of the handle of the rear door, but there was no foothold so he fell to the ground.

Tears swelled in Niamh's eyes and slowly and reluctantly flowed down her face. And then she started to run. Belatedly, she had realized that she did not know where the new house was. The van rounded the corner of B Block, but Niamh kept on running. She ran and ran until she reached the Cross Gate. She was just in time to see the van pick up speed and disappear. With it went all hope of seeing her friend again.

"Do you draw on your own experiences for your writing?" was a question Niamh was frequently asked.

"You great pillock, everyone draws on their own life when creating a work of fiction. Surely, it's self-evident. You can only experience human existence through living your own life so it must follow that whatever you produce is a product of that life, the life that has shaped your ways of seeing and doing.

Simple?

Don't look at me as though I've failed the artistic test because I use what I've heard, observed, learned. For Christ's sake, didn't Joyce examine every atom of his life and use it as material for his writings? *Dubliners*, A *Portrait of the Artist as a Young Man*, and, to the best of my knowledge, *Ulysses* and *Finnegan's Wake*.

And so did Sean O'Casey.

And so did Edna O'Brien.

And so did …

But you could go on in that vein forever."

Although this is what she wanted to say she refrained from doing so. What she actually said was, "Yes, I do, although the details are, of course, fictitious. But the themes that draw me, that I wish to explore, arise out of my having lived in a particular place at a particular time."

"But surely there are universal themes that concern writers throughout the ages, regardless of time or place?"

"Goes without saying, it's called the human condition. Yes, I know that that phrase opens up a can of worms and that we could talk all day and all night about its precise meaning, but to move on, the genre, the form, the style, are dictated, or at least influenced, by where and when you live, and the pain and joy of your life will push its way through all of these. So to answer the question, yes, I draw on my own experiences for my writing."

*

"Not a sinner,
Not a soul,
Just yourself.

Not a sinner,
Not a soul,
Just yourself.

You're fooolin'
No one, just yourself.

You're fooolin'
No one, just yourself.

You're a great big fat liar,
You're in a state of denial,
You're fooolin'
No one, just yourself."

"I know there are writers who write their own lives over and over, but I've never done that." A well-known writer was holding forth on Radio 4 about his latest work. "To make a career out of your own life," he went on, "you need to have experienced great sorrow, but I have had a life of good fortune and happiness so therefore I look for inspiration outside of myself."

Bollocks.

But hold on.

Maybe he had a point.

If one had lived the life to which he attested and then wrote about it, wouldn't he bore the pants off everyone? How many people could hope to identify with his tale of unrelieved delight?

But, if he'd had a mother, father, brother, sister, wife or child, or any combination of these, surely somewhere, at sometime, he had felt pain, had felt sadness? Could you be part of all those relationships without suffering? Look at poor W.B., crying into his coddle because his grandma was ill.

Unless, of course, you were an unfeeling monster.

But could you be a hard-hearted swine and an artist as well?

Probably.

> Not a sinner,
> Not a soul,
> Just yourself.
>
> Not a sinner,
> Not a soul,
> Just yourself.
>
> You're fooolin'
> No one, just yourself.

*

She needed to write. Wanted to find a quiet corner, gaze at the world and jot down anything that came to mind, but she was in Dublin where the adage, 'There's no tax on talk', was taken as gospel, so asking for quiet was like asking for silence in the modern version of a madhouse – the stock exchange. Joyce, Beckett, Casey, et al did not leave Dublin because of the stifling society created by the British, the catholic church, et al — it was the garrulous nature of the people which had driven them away: they had wearied of a population that was incapable of shutting its gob.

*

She walked along Aungier Street, past Whitefriar Street Church and remembered how often she'd nipped into its vast interior to kneel before St. Valentine's gruesome monument, (bits and pieces of him in a black and gold casket and a small vessel tinged with his blood) begging him to make the love of her life (whoever that happened to be at a given time) love her in return. But time and again the snivelling trickster had let her down. Instead of the handsome young man she had prayed for, he had sent her, time and again, a gangly youth, sprouting pimples and wispy hairs on a weak chin.

The young were weird: obsessed with the grisly, the macabre, and the church did little to discourage them with its ubiquitous images of Christ on the cross, thorns driven into his skull, cruel nails driven into his hands and feet, thick globules of blood oozing from his flesh. And pictures of Jesus with an exposed heart, a flaming glowing trophy, gouged from the cavity of his chest! The church's bloody aesthetic had a coarsening effect. Because of it, in the name of lust, she'd been prepared to prostrate herself in front of the partial remains of a man.

Catholic doctrine, for all its cant about peace and love, glorified violence and cannibalism: all that blood and gore and all that guff about being cleansed by eating and drinking the body and blood of Christ.

Had not a Dublin man written Dracula?

Only trouble was, he wasn't a catholic.

But that didn't matter a toss. Who could avoid the reach of the church in this city?

Enough said.

Case closed.

Not quite.

If she ever saw her mother again she'd ask her opinion on the matter.

Having strolled up Wexford Street and Camden Street she had lunched at a café next to Kelly's Corner. Sitting on a high stool directly facing the window, she had a good view of the busy scene outside. Straight on at the traffic lights led to Harrington Street; a right into Synge Street led to the renowned boys' school.

Many years previously, to the delight and pride of her parents, her eldest brother had passed an exam that allowed him to attend this prestigious academy — an amazing feat for a boy from the barracks. And her mother never tired of telling the neighbours just how amazing it was. As far as the young Niamh could gather (and she was relying on overheard snippets of hushed conversation between her parents which ceased as soon as she came within earshot) after two years he was required to sit another exam. Success would mean a scholarship that would pay for the remainder of his secondary education. But the unimaginable happened. The boy who had always performed brilliantly in exams failed to achieve the required marks. Unless her parents could pay the fees he was sunk, would have to leave the school.

Her brother was baffled. He knew for certain sure that his marks were higher than those of another scholar and that that scholar had been awarded a scholarship. So her parents huddled in the kitchen talking and talking. The talking gave rise to unprecedented action. Her father plucked up courage and made an appointment to see the senior christian brother, donned his best clothes and went to argue his son's case.

To no avail.

It seemed (and Niamh may have misunderstood; she was ten years old and eavesdropping) that had her father been in a position to make a generous donation to the school her brother's bacon could have been saved.

But no could do.

So no deal.

The entire episode presented her mother with a serious dilemma. Should she believe that her brilliant first-born was not so brilliant after all? Should she believe that the church in which she had believed all her life was not to be believed in?

She hit on a way to settle the matter. She decided to do a novena. Every Friday for nine weeks, as soon as she had packed the children off to school, she put the baby in the pram and walked up Leinster Road, along Harold's Cross Road, Lower Kimmage Road and into Mount Argus Church where she knelt and prayed fervently for guidance.

But she failed in her desire to believe in the integrity of the church.

And for one simple reason.

She knew her son had been robbed.

*

Many years later a young priest, fresh to Birmingham from County Wexford, decided he would assuage his loneliness by visiting parishioners as lonely as himself and had the misfortune to knock on Niamh's door.

He had a cup of tea. "Ah, go on, Father, just a cup in your hand."

He marvelled at the coincidence that Niamh's father came from the same county as himself. "Imagine that. Isn't it a small world?" and settled down to spend a pleasant half-hour away from the parish priest who had left Ireland thirty years previously and who, if the young priest was any judge, had been drunk ever since.

To save her life Niamh couldn't afterwards recall how they had hit on the disgrace of her brother's missed opportunity; whatever the reason she'd chucked a beamer at the young priest, aimed it right at his nut. She regaled him with the details of the scandal, prepared herself to rebut his defence of the indefensible. But the poor eejit didn't attempt to deny that such a thing could happen. He actually tried to explain the logic of the situation. It went something like this.

Her brother, though doubtless intelligent, was the eldest of a large poor family and a place at a prestigious school would be wasted on him. In denying her brother his place the christian brothers had done him and his family a favour. Yes, the scholarship would pay for fees and books, but there were bound to be extra expenses that they would struggle to meet and her brother would be humiliated, constantly, by this state of affairs. And, besides, it was doubtful if the family could have afforded to keep him in full-time education until he reached the age of eighteen, so a place would definitely have been wasted on him. She couldn't deny that, surely?

She could and did. Her voice was calm and deliberate as she began her rebuttal.

"Please correct me if I'm wrong father," she said. "It seems to me that you are defending the charade my brother endured. He was invited to sit a competitive examination to obtain a scholarship that would pay for his secondary education, was successful in obtaining the necessary marks to win a place and was robbed of that place because he came from a family which was too poor to bribe the school. He was denied an opportunity to avail himself of the best education the country had to offer, denied the prestige this would bring because the fabulously wealthy catholic church would not grant him a sufficiently generous scholarship to pay for the extras he might need. You are a priest and you are defending hypocrisy, dishonesty and downright robbery, not to mention cruelty. Your way of thinking almost destroyed my mother."

The young priest was on his feet.

Retreating towards the door.

*

After lunching at Kelly's Corner she had strolled along Richmond Street towards the canal. This, she had decided, would be her last port of call for the day. She was knackered. The distance she'd walked was not great, but tripping back to the past was proving to be a killer.

She supposed that everyone reached a stage where they tried to make sense of their lives, but she wondered if the process was most difficult for those who had left their native land: those who, in the flush of youth and ignorance, had torn from the soil of their heritage the roots of generations, left without a backward glance only to find, as the years passed, that native soil keeps a tenacious hold, refuses to be shaken off. Joyce himself couldn't wait to break free of Ireland: had run off with Nora Barnacle. But Ireland had proved a jealous mistress and would not let him be.

Niamh wanted to tell all the young immigrants who passed her in the streets about the perils of their situation: about how, for many years — much longer then they could imagine — they would live split lives. Physically they would live here in Dublin, but in their heads, their hearts, their dreams, they would live in the place of their birth. She wanted to tell them about the pain of separation. The feeling of exclusion which cut like a knife through the heart that came with missing births, baptisms, parties, weddings and Christmases — all the celebrations which bind a family together. She wanted to tell them how proof of their existence would disappear as a membrane of absence grew over the space they had once occupied within their family, of how the existence of their own children would constitute an endless rebuke for the cultural and familial loss that had been inflicted upon them. Her three children, (Tim, Jessica, Harry) now well into adulthood, continued to travel the globe in ever-widening circles and she felt powerless to urge them home. After all, theirs were the shallow roots of just one generation. She had broken a lineage of centuries.

But even if she could tell her children and these immigrants all of these things, it would make no difference. They would think her a mad old woman who had lost touch with the reality of the modern world. People were on the move as never before. It was easier to travel; there were so many ways to keep in contact — by letter, phone, email, Skype. Yes, all of these, and even seeing loved ones on computer and on new-fangled telephones.

But what of holding:
Touching:
Being?

*

She sat on the wall of the canal at Portobello Bridge. She was on home territory now, within spitting distance of where she had grown up.

Incessant waves of memory pounded inside her head. Walking by the canal the nursing home St. Ultan's Hospital The Salvation Army The Children of Mary the car factory Radio Eireann years of walking backwards and forwards over the bridge towards town over the bridge towards home mother father brothers friends backwards forwards backwards forwards.

She took Joyce's book from her bag and stroked the cover absentmindedly.

"You like reading?" Niamh glanced towards her left and into the smiling face of an elderly man. His face was a network of wrinkles, but his brown eyes were clear and challenging. "You like reading?" he asked again.

"Yes, yes I do," she said, hoping he would go away.

"I like reading too," he said, in heavily accented English. "I read very much. You are a very beautiful lady," he added.

Christ! Niamh thought, gripping the book to her chest.

"You have children?"

"Yes, I have three children."

"I have four children and I have a grandson who like to read. He will be a doctor. He is very clever boy."

As she sat clutching her book he told her of his life. He had left Costa Rica and joined the American merchant fleet. He had sailed the world. He had stayed in England and then moved to Ireland. He no longer had a wife.

"You are married?" he asked.

"My husband ... my husband died."

"I am sorry," he said, his voice deep with sympathy. "I will meet you tomorrow and I will take you to Salsa."

"I shan't be here tomorrow," she lied, and he burst into song. He bent down, put his face next to hers and sang a tender love song in his native Spanish. His voice conveyed the longing of the truly lonely and it pierced Niamh's heart.

"Thank you," she said when he had finished.

"You are sure you will not be here tomorrow?" he asked.

"No, I shan't be here tomorrow."

He raised his hand in farewell and Niamh concentrated on the blurb on the back cover of *Ulysses*, but the print swam and floated as she tried to hold back the tears.

She felt a movement and looked up once again. He was back. This time he serenaded her in English, offering a rendition of "And I Love You So". She smiled her thanks, rose from the wall and left him.

*

She caught a number fourteen bus into town, a number seven to Merrion and enjoyed a cream tea in the hotel restaurant.

Back in her room she sat by the window, looking at the shimmering sweep of Dublin Bay as the waves ebbed away from the sea wall. Ten minutes later she tore her gaze from the peaceful scene, moved to the writing table and wrote for some time in a notebook, then lay on the bed, opened *Ulysses* and promptly fell asleep.

Her first viewing of *Hamlet* almost finished her with Shakespeare for life.

Her English teacher at The High School of Commerce Rathmines, one Miss Brown, who spent all her energies being merry and flirtatious with male members of staff so had little stamina left for her students, said it was high time she exposed her uncouth charges to some real culture. Without preparation of any kind, she herded them into the college hall and forced them to sit for hours and hours watching a grainy copy of a black and white film in which an actor in tights, a blonde mat stuck to his head, pranced about on the ramparts of a castle, talked to a skull and, finally, to the relief and joy of the conscripted audience, died a painful death.

Years later, after a more enjoyable experience at the Birmingham Rep (and having seen many other performances, including one with Kenneth Branagh at the RSC) *Hamlet* became her favourite Shakespeare play.

The posh twit from *Hi di Hi* had played the lead at the Rep in a dreamy troubled manner that appealed to Niamh. At that time she had not read the text and was astounded and delighted at how many lines of dialogue seemed like old friends: 'To be or not to be', 'Alas poor Yorick' (courtesy of a cigar advertisement), 'Thou hast cleft my heart in twain', 'Get thee to a nunnery', (very popular with young Irish men flexing their libidinous muscles when she was growing up. As they uttered the words, the silly young fools were gripped by a frisson of excitement), and the one that really stood the test of time for some deluded males, 'Frailty, thy name is woman'.

In subsequent years, the more she studied the play the more elusive it became. The shifting sands of Shakespeare's plot and characterization shifted the meaning with each reading.

Hamlet was a young man justifiably traumatized by the death of his father and the hasty re-marriage of his mother: justifiably suspicious of his uncle.

Hamlet was a cruel, self-obsessed, conniving shit who drove his young lover to suicide and sent his friends to certain death: a son with an unhealthy affection for his mother, a coward unable to strike the fatal blow when the opportunity arose.

Hamlet was a prince who inspired love and affection in Horatio and the good citizens of Denmark: a young man who paid the ultimate price for being in the wrong place at the wrong time.

Hamlet was all of the above.

Shakespeare, it had been widely accepted, had scoured the chronicles of Holinshed for his plots and characters. But Stephen Dedalus had not fallen for that one.

Having enjoyed forty winks Niamh had just read his disquisition on the play in *Ulysses* and had found it amazingly illuminating. The characterizations, the events — the intrigue, betrayals, sexual argy-bargy — all, according to Stephen, had been taken from the bard's family life. They'd been a right shower; that lot in Stratford-upon-Avon in the sixteenth century. But Shakespeare did not forget. He stored it all up and then stitched them up good and proper. He set it all down, wrote up their treacheries, their deceptions, laid bare their foibles, shortcomings, weaknesses. And five centuries later their story unfolded, fresh as ever, night after night, across the stages of the world.

Unlike the pillock on Radio 4 it seemed the Bard had not fought shy of using his own life as the basis for his work. So his was another name to add to the list.

*

How many of Joyce's family and friends had recognized themselves in his work? A fair question. How well had he disguised his characters? No doubt had she the time and inclination she could find a detailed academic disquisition on the subject.

She had not read much of *Ulysses*, but the difficulties she had experienced at previous attempts still beset her. She would need all the help she could get to unravel its meaning. Apart from the opening passage and Stephen's treatise on *Hamlet*, she was finding the text impenetrable. She was reading a chapter where language itself seemed to disintegrate, to fall apart — was pared to the bone — not up to the task of explaining the world. It resonated with the rhythms she associated with Beckett. (Having sat through *Krapp's Last Tape*, *Not I*, and four more of his shorts in one evening at The Other Place in Stratford, she thought herself something of an authority.) As to meaning — it was beyond her.

But if language had reached its limits early in the twentieth-century what did that mean for what had transpired since? Was there anything left to say? Was what Joyce had written intended to be the last word on the subject of the reality of human existence? Was he making the point that silence is the only reasonable, rational response to a world drunk on violence? But if that were the case why had he written *Finnegans Wake*?

And speaking of Dubliners, she had Sean O'Casey to thank for her life-long love of theatre, for her desire to grapple with the works of Shakespeare, Ibsen, Beckett, *et al.*

*

Her first experience of theatre (apart from the school productions where she had appeared as a mermaid in *Pearl The Fisher-maiden* and St. Bernadette in a tableaux — chosen because, as a ten year old, Sister Herman thought she looked like a fourteen year old consumptive) was a production of Sean O'Casey's *Juno and the Paycock* at The Shack in Portobello Barracks.

On stage were people like her, speaking in an accent like hers, using language as she used it and heard it spoken every day. She was entranced, despite the fact that she was sitting on a hard bench, surrounded by her brothers and jeering young soldiers, disappointed that their usual Thursday night film had been replaced by an amateur production of a great playwright's masterpiece.

She had been amazed, puzzled and unnerved at being allowed to accompany her brothers to The Shack on that occasion because, situated in the military section of the barracks, it was usually out of bounds to her — a no-go area after dark. But that evening her mother had virtually forced her and her brothers out the door.

"Take her, take her, take her," her mother had urged Niamh's elder brother.

"But she's not allowed. It's down the barracks. Daddy doesn't let her go there," Daniel protested. And it was true. In those unenlightened times it was only girls who were protected from predators. It was some years before horrified parents realized that whilst they had marshalled their forces to protect the front door, the rear was also vulnerable.

Niamh held tightly to her brother's hand. When they breasted the Band Room she looked back to wave goodbye. Her mother's usual healthy complexion was pale, white as snow, her face twisted in pain. Niamh tugged at her brother's hand, but he tightened his grip and pulled her along.

*

Two and a half hours later as they made their way home, taking care to avoid the Nissan huts behind the sergeants' mess where soldiers with mysterious illnesses were billeted, her brothers grumbling all the while about being robbed of seeing one of their cowboy heroes in the weekly follier-upper — Roy Rogers and his horse Trigger, Gene Autry and Champion The Wonder Horse, Tom Mix, or the black-leather-clad, Lash Laroo, who used his vicious whip to uphold the forces for good — and instead had to sit through "a load of shite", Niamh thought again about her mother's pale face.

When they opened the door the flat was strangely quiet. Her mother didn't come to greet them. Niamh ran to the kitchen to tell her about the wonderful play she'd seen, about Joxer Daly who was just like Mr. Nolan and Captain Boyle who was the spit of Mr. Foster, but the kitchen was deserted, everything tidied away, no cups of cocoa ready, no great wedges of bread spread with creamy butter.

They heard a door open and ran into the living room. A strange woman, wearing a white apron over a navy dress, was standing by the bedroom door.

"Where's our mammy?" Daniel demanded.

"Your mammy's sleeping, *a stór*," the woman said, a wide smile lighting her face, "so you've got to be good children and get yourselves to bed as quietly as possible."

"Who are you?" Paul asked.

"I'm the midwife. I'm looking after your mammy until your daddy gets home."

"What's wrong with her?"

"She had a bad stomach ache, but she's better now. Get yourselves to bed and you'll see her in the morning."

"I want my daddy," Niamh said.

"I'll tell him when he comes home." The woman turned back towards the bedroom. "Remember children, as quiet as mice, now."

*

Many years passed before Niamh learnt that their mother had waived the strict rule that forbade her young daughter access to The Shack because she had, almost four months into her pregnancy, begun to miscarry late that afternoon. Unable to contact her husband and reluctant to alarm her children, she had bundled them out of the house, alerted a neighbour and sat astride a bucket as her spurting blood flushed her infant from her womb.

    She had done all of this without painkillers and had endured a D&C in her own home, without anaesthetic, rather than be taken into hospital and away from her children.

Niamh was up and out early the next morning, carrying her book. The heavy tome weighed her down, but she had become attached to it, become almost superstitious about leaving it behind. It was her talisman, her good luck charm, although she could not think from what it might protect her.

She stayed on the bus until it reached O'Connell Street, disembarked and walked across the road to North Earl Street. She stood for a few moments looking at a statue of Joyce. There he was, confident and debonair, one foot crossed over the other, leaning casually on a walking stick. The bronze Joyce, head held high, hat perched at a rakish angle, looked completely relaxed and at home, exuding a sense of belonging which had been denied him in life. Even in death Dubliners were miserly in their esteem for the man. 'The Prick with the Stick' was the *sobriquet* local wits had conferred on his statue. This mockery did not prevent them basking in the glow of his writings which, they liked to believe, gave credence to their favourite self-image — that of the articulate, intelligent Dublin wit.

*

Just after ten o'clock she was back where she had left off the day before, on Portobello Bridge, looking south along Lower Rathmines Road, the Dublin Mountains, beloved of Beckett, blue and misty in the distance.

She was standing on Canal Road next to the bridge. In the distance the Town Hall clock chimed the quarter hour. Once again she was bombarded by memories. On this very spot, every weekend, The Salvation Army had blasted their message about the lord at the people of Dublin. The people of Dublin knew all they needed to know about the lord, but, being suckers for music, they would stop awhile to listen to the soldiers, dressed in their navy uniforms and silly caps and bonnets, silver instruments glinting in the sun, make music that could strip the skin from the inner ear.

Niamh was relieved to see that Portobello House, on the opposite side of the road, had escaped the developers. Opened in 1807 as The Grand Canal Hotel it had become a private nursing home in 1898 and continued as such throughout her time in Dublin. Jack Yeats, painter, and brother of the poet, had lived there for many years — a useless bit of information she could share with W.B.

The building held a strange fascination for the young Niamh as she passed it every day on her journey into the city centre. Its grand stucco edifice and imposing portico stood away from the main thoroughfare and overlooked the canal; rows of windows shrouded in dense blinds added a remote and mysterious aura. Her greatest fear had been that she might collapse close-by and be admitted for treatment. She imagined that once inside her family would never find her. She was convinced, on no evidence at all, that few of its patients came out alive.

*

Right.

She had to decide how circular her circular route would be. Should she fan out from the original starting point of O'Connell Street or from her starting point each day? That gave her two immediate choices: the first would take her along Rathmines Road, the latter along Grove Road and a canal-side stroll.

She decided on the latter.

She waited for the traffic lights to change and crossed over. The four swans that her brother Daniel had said were the children of Lir were, of course, no longer in residence. In her memory they floated majestically backwards and forwards, ducking their heads beneath the cold black water in search of food. She hated when, on resurfacing, they stretched their long necks towards her and fixed her with eyes as black and cold as the water in which they swam.

Daniel had heightened her anxiety. "After nine hundred years in the water they'll come onto dry land," he had told her. "They'll turn into really old people with long hair and all their skin will fall off their bodies. They'll hook their claws into children, especially girls, and drag them into the water and drown them, so they will."

"How long have they been in the water?"

"Don't know."

But the birds had gifted a sight that even Daniel's morbid imaginings couldn't destroy. One summer evening as Niamh walked towards home, the beating wings of two swans lifted their bodies above the water and, in a great rush, they took flight towards the orange ball of the setting sun.

But it seemed that swans had given up on the Grand Canal, at least on this stretch. Now, apart from waving reeds, clumps of litter and green slime, the water was empty.

She kept walking. To her left new flats had sprung up. No more than five years old, already they showed signs of wear and tear with crumbling plaster and shoddy wood.

She was approaching the Canal Gate of what had once been known as Portobello Barracks (it had been renamed in 1952 in honour of Cathal Brugha, one of the commanders of the 1916 rising), the place where she had been born and where she had lived until she left Ireland. She had rarely used this entrance as a young woman — it led directly onto the officers' quarters and tennis courts — uncomfortable territory for a corporal's daughter.

The garrison church was tucked away behind the policeman's hut at the Canal Gate. Most families from married quarters chose not to attend this church, leaving it to the officers, their stuck-up families and the unmarried soldiers billeted nearby. Instead, ordinary soldiers and their kin escaped to civvy-street and the parish church in Rathmines. But there were two reasons why this practice might be abandoned — to hear the military choir sing Gregorian chant that filled every crevice of the church with a sound so deep and resonant that the congregation was in danger of bursting from the joy of it.

The other reason was more mundane and expedient. As they grew older and their sins more sexual in nature the youngsters of the barracks discovered that army chaplains, hardened by the confessions of young soldiers, were less likely to be outraged by what they heard than their counterparts in the parish church.

*

Niamh looked through the heavy metal gates. To the right stood the hut that her father had often manned; straight ahead a long road stretched as far as the eye could see. She knew it reached all the way to the Cross Gate; the boundary between the military barracks and married quarters.

Alongside the hut three young soldiers, in light combat uniforms and black berets, stood chatting and laughing. The soldier nearest the gate removed a beret and a tousled mass of dark hair escaped. The young woman threw back her head and ran languid fingers through her hair. With a wave of her hand she walked away from her laughing colleagues, left them gazing at the movement of her swivelling hips, which even the baggy combats could not disguise.

*

She had reached Harold's Cross Bridge with its stone carving of the young Robert Emmet who had been hanged by the British in 1802 for having the temerity to stage a rebellion.

She would take a left turn along Harold's Cross Road and another left onto Leinster Road. It was quite a trek for an old bird like herself, but she would stop at Rosie O'Grady's for refreshments.

Niamh hadn't realized she was singing aloud the lilting song that paid homage to the bold Rosie until another voice joined in close by.

"A grand song that," a man said, his eyes twinkling and blue beneath bushy eyebrows. "Did you know it was written by a woman?" He didn't wait for her reply.

"Yes indeed it was, Maude Nugent, in the nineteenth century and it was sung by Betty Grable in a film in 1943." And off he went, singing at the top of his voice.

*

She ordered a lunch of bacon, cabbage and mashed potatoes, washed it down with water, and tucked into a generous slice of hot apple tart and custard.

The pub was busy and noisy and she had to share a table with three Polish men who'd popped in to quench the raging thirst of a morning's work on a building site.

She ordered coffee, took her book from her bag confident, for once, of an uninterrupted read. As she read she marvelled at Joyce's mastery. Having demolished language he reconstructed it, utilized its rich diversity, its voluptuousness, to lampoon, mercilessly, the arrogance and cruelty of the colonizer and the overblown, self-important impotence of the colonized. Layer upon layer of allusion, irony, vivid imagery, wit and humour danced off the page.

"It is a good book, you think?" The young man sitting next to her asked.

"It is a very good book." She glanced at him and then back to the page she was reading.

"Joyce, he was a genius."

"He was."

"I have read it in Polish."

Her mind buckled, trying in vain to imagine soft Dublin vowels rendered in that consonant-laden language.

"And you understood what was going on?"

"Of course."

"Begob, sure you must be a feckin' genius yourself."

"I am sorry; I do not understand what you say."

"I rest my case."

But Niamh had spoken too hastily.

"I understand Joyce," the young man said. "We Poles, we have much experience of the alienation of Jews." When Niamh did not answer, he added. "You are here on wrong day."

"What do you mean?"

"It is not Bloom's day. It is not sixteenth of June."

"No, it's not the sixteenth of June."

"Sixteenth of June is my mother's name day, so I remember Bloom's day."

"Right."

*

Reluctant to leave the pub after the young Polish men bade her a courteous good-bye, she lingered over the ruins of her meal.

So far her musings on the past had failed to yield anything to explain her nightly horrors. She couldn't decide whether to be pleased or disappointed. It was a past like that of most people, she supposed, with moments of joy, anguish, the ordinary and extraordinary intertwined.

She ruminated on the score so far.

Returned Exile 0: Personal Demons 1: would possibly be fair at this juncture.

But the next stage of her journey would take her into the heartland of her childhood and, suddenly, she felt frightened of what she might discover.

Her route was all wrong.

She should have skirted the outer edges of Dublin, roamed along the coast from Sandymount to Killiney, soaked up the briny atmosphere before heading back to the city. But, no, she had to march straight through the briar patch.

Well, she wasn't ready.

So feck it.

She would walk from Harold's Cross to Rathmines and catch a bus by the Town Hall into town.

Tomorrow she would go to the sea.

Terraced houses stood, assured and solid, on either side of Leinster Road, confident of their elegance and durability. They had been the backdrop to her childhood ramblings and she loved the uniformity of their clean, sturdy lines and the contrasting details of individual houses — the delicate tracery of fanlights, the brightly painted doors, the intricate ironwork of the railings which enclosed small gardens.

She wondered at the comfort to be derived from the durability of buildings: how their longevity made us feel secure and protected despite the fact that it doesn't matter a toss whether a structure of bricks and mortar survives us, doesn't change the basic fact that we are mortal, that we will die. Perhaps we put our faith in houses because even the most humble of us needs a monument: needs to leave behind proof that we once existed, evidence of what we attained. Or perhaps we want to fool ourselves that we are as durable as our buildings.

Not everyone was interested in bricks and mortar. Joyce, who had spent his childhood moving from house to house as the number of his siblings increased and his father drank away the family inheritance, had little interest in property. In adulthood, with the exception of producing a large family, he had followed his father's example; he drank heavily and moved to a succession of flats around Europe. But he had created a monument greater than any building. The works of literary genius he had left behind would outlast most modern structures.

*

She was halfway down Leinster Road. The bench at the corner of Grosvenor Square had been removed. She had been depending on it for a rest. In its absence she leant against a garden wall. If she followed the road for another twenty yards and took a right down the narrow alleyway of Grosvenor Lane she would arrive at the married-quarters gate of Cathal Brugha Barracks. She was close to home. But she would not venture — not today.

Behind her, and to the right, the noble pile of the Longford estate had been demolished.

Good riddance to bad rubbish.

And so say all of us.

A terrace of pseudo-Georgian houses had replaced it.

Just the ticket.

Lord Longford's estate had been both an affront and a challenge to the kids from the barracks. Although he took his name from an Irish county they knew he was an English lord and that was enough to earn their loathing. To add insult to injury his gardeners grew a lush crop of fruit on Irish soil and protected it within a fortress of stonewalls. Nothing for it but to breach the defences and take back what is rightfully ours — was the cry of each generation of boys from the barracks when they reached a certain age. So raiding parties were sent out to box the fox, and plentiful apples were had, and many suffered griping stomach pains.

*

"She said she was going to have an abortion. She just sat there and announced to us all that she was off to London the next day. Can you credit it? Imagine having the brazen effrontery, the impudent audacity to say a thing like that," the woman spluttered to a halt before starting up again. "It's that Cadden one's fault. She started it all, here in Rathmines: right over there in that very house."

Niamh followed the woman's gaze as she nodded her head towards a solid terrace on the right "A trollop she was: a black-hearted trollop".

"Arrah, sure times change, I suppose," said her companion, "and sure sometimes it's hard to change with them."

"Change! Why should we change? What's right is right, and the sanctity of human life must be defended."

The bus stopped and the women disembarked. Niamh sighed with relief. Nurse Cadden would turn in her grave if she knew that Irish women were still denied the right to control their own fertility. Not that Mamie Cadden had been a saint — far from it, but fair's fair, there was a great demand for her work and it was a demand created, to a large extent, by catholic teaching.

Niamh had become aware of the black-hearted trollop's existence through the whisperings of her parents; she hadn't a clue what was going on, but she knew it wasn't good.

"Oh, my god, she didn't. Oh, my god, how could a nurse do that? Niamh, go out and play, this minute."

"A woman's body dumped in Hume Street in the middle of the night! Oh, that Cadden one is evil, so she is! Niamh, don't stand where adults are talking, go out this minute."

"But what drives women to go to her, do you think? Sure they must be desperate." Niamh was struck by the wistful note in her mother's voice, before she added the familiar refrain, "Niamh, go and see where your brother is. Now, I said."

The image of a monstrous woman, dragging a body in the murky darkness of early morning near Stephen's Green, had stayed with Niamh, and a few years ago, by chance, she had come across the name once again and discovered that Nurse Cadden had operated very close to where she had grown up. She had owned a property on Lower Rathmines Road — the very road Niamh was now travelling along — and had run a maternity nursing home from the premises. She also ran a profitable sideline in placing unwanted babies and aborting unwanted foetuses.

Niamh wondered if any of the women from the barracks had visited Nurse Cadden. With families of eight, nine, ten commonplace, they could have benefited from her services, but they probably couldn't afford them. Certainly poor Mrs. Cleary who had lived in the block next to hers could not. Babies popped from her like peas from pods. Even as a child Niamh wondered how Mrs. Cleary could keep going through the horror of her life. She knew from her own experience the difficulties of living cheek by jowl with a large number of people in a small space, but her mother was quick, intelligent, able, and through her heroic efforts her family survived and prospered. Mrs.

Cleary was slow and bewildered — she had endured so many pregnancies that her entire body was bloated like a watermelon — belly, arms, feet, face, permanently swollen. Little ones clung to her apron, her hands, legs: anywhere they could get a hold. And the amazing thing was that she smiled through it all. And her husband smiled too: a leering senseless grin that made the flesh on Niamh's adolescent body creep every time he turned his gaze on her as she passed him in the road.

But Mrs. Cleary's smile was not an expression of pleasure. She smiled because she was not the full shilling so had little grasp on the reality of her life; was incapable of comparing her lot with anyone else's. She had a mental age of about twelve. But, apparently, there was no law, civil or ecclesiastical, to save her from her fate.

But the law, criminal and ecclesiastical, had no difficulty in dealing with Nurse Cadden. She was sentenced to a year's hard labour on a charge of abandoning a baby by the side of the road in County Meath. When she was released from prison she continued to ply her illegal trade and was soon sentenced to another five years, but on her release she was at it again. Catholic teaching, which forbade the use of contraception, thrust an unending supply of customers in her direction. Although a qualified midwife, she was forced to work under poor conditions so it was only a matter of time before disaster struck. The body of one of her patients was found on the pavement in Hume Street and she was tried for murder, was sentenced to death, but her sentence was commuted to life imprisonment.

Nurse Cadden held much incriminating evidence on many good catholics so a way had to be found to undermine her credibility completely and catholic Ireland was up to the job.

Never let it be said.

Undaunted we proceed.

On no account should her voice be heard.

Certify her.

Declare the bitch insane.

And they did.

And she was sent to Dundrum Lunatic Asylum where she died after two years' incarceration.

*

The bus travelled along Rathmines Road and Niamh caught a glimpse of the imposing green dome of the parish church where she had been baptised, made her first communion, her confirmation and was married: where, time and again, her head had rebounded off the tiled floor as she conked out, faint from fasting.

She glanced quickly to her left and up the dark, tree-lined avenue towards the Military Road entrance to the barracks, back again and straight on towards Portobello Bridge, her starting point that morning.

She had come full circle: had, in this one day, circled the backdrop to the early part of her life.

*

A message from W.B. was waiting at the hotel. Could she make it to the Gresham for dinner at seven if he sent a taxi?

"It's far from the Gresham you were reared."

"Who does tha' one think she is?"

"Jaysus, she doesn't half smell herself."

All the local put-downs rattled in her head, but she didn't care. She wasn't going to miss an opportunity to dine at one of the most famous hotels in the city, to experience a first at her age.

She would have a bath, read awhile and then dress with care for her night out.

*

Gerty MacDowell was a piece of work. If all the young ones in Dublin were like her it was no wonder Mamie Cadden's services had been so sought after. What a little rip! Egging a man on like that. And it all done by a glance, by a movement, by the way she arranged herself on the rocks. And her letting her imagination soar, writing the story of Bloom, creating the man she dreamed of. And he devouring her with his eyes and bringing himself off there on Sandymount Strand.

And not a word spoken.

Maybe Joyce was right. Maybe the best encounters are silent encounters. Language can confuse the issue; distort meaning. And perhaps we create the partner we crave: fix on some poor sod and convince ourselves that they are handsome, beautiful, kind, generous, sexually rampant, and then despise them for not being any or all of these things. Perhaps it is our fate, in matters of the heart, to create our own unhappiness, our discontent.

Now she was reading an episode that encompassed a variety of styles: part of it was written in archaic English and reminded her of *The Wife of Bath's Prologue and Tale*. And Joyce was on about motherhood and pregnancy and the pain of childbirth, but apart from that she couldn't make head or tail of it, couldn't understand to what purpose he was writing.

She willed herself to concentrate, to keep going, but her eyelids quivered and drooped; she tried to hold her head upright, but it wobbled a little and then fell forward onto her chest. The book dropped from her hands as she succumbed to blissful sleep.

Tommy Doherty was in love: publicly, unashamedly in love, which was in the nature of things.

Unfortunately for Mrs. Doherty, Mr. Doherty was not in love with her. However, sympathy for Tommy's wife was not universal among the women of Cathal Brugha Barracks.

"I don't know why that one is moanin' and wailin'," Nuala Murray said. "She should get down on her knees and thank god that he's got someone else to paw and maul."

"I wish my Jack would find a mistress," Lena O'Neill sighed, "maybe then I could have a good night's sleep."

"I wouldn't hold out much hope of tha' happening," Áine Foley sneered, "sure if a hot-blooded woman made eyes at your Jack he'd piss himself."

"No man likes a woman with a coarse tongue," sniffed Lena.

Áine threw back her head and laughed. "I wouldn't bet on that *a leanbh*, because you'd be certain to lose money, so you would."

*

Surrounded as the inhabitants of married quarters were by civilians — the residents of Leinster Road to the south, Grosvenor Square to the west and Rathmines Road to the east, they had developed a siege mentality. The fact that the affluent people of

Rathmines looked down their snooty noses at ordinary soldiers and their families, did not want them living in their midst, reinforced the insularity of the military families still further. Thrown together because of their men's work and isolated from the wider society, they were a close-knit community, with all the strengths and weaknesses that this entailed.

The compound housed seventy families and everyone knew everyone else's business. Almost without exception, talking about their neighbours was like eating and drinking for women who rarely moved beyond the confines of the barracks. With children in school and household chores attended to they would slip next door to obtain an update or to embellish local gossip.

With sixty-nine experienced spies on the case Tommy Doherty knew he couldn't hope to keep his liaison secret so he decided to brazen it out. Throughout the summer of 1953 Tommy parked his Morris Minor Estate at the end of B Block, beeped his horn and waited for his ladylove to descend the stairs. On cue, Francie O'Casey emerged from her flat, tottering on five inch heels and, under the scandalized gaze of the mothers who sat on their front door-steps, watching their children play and enjoying the evening sun, she made her way with much aplomb to meet her heart's delight.

"There's one born every minute," Breda Carey said to Maggie Cronin.

"That one will suck him in and blow him out in bubbles, so she will," said Maggie, "and he deserves all he gets."

"It's his kids I feel sorry for," Brenda Bolger shouted so that Francie would hear. "Anyone who hurts little chiselurs should burn in hell."

Francie answered with a more pronounced swing of her hips and a flick of her long brown hair.

"I'm teaching her to drive," was Tommy's story. "Sure wouldn't any neighbour do the same?"

Tommy and Francie kept the barracks amused throughout the summer. On balmy evenings the passion wagon, windows covered by yellow curtains, Tommy at the wheel, his ample jowls supported by a coordinating yellow cravat, wended its way from B Block, through the Cross Gate and out of sight.

Speculation as to what actually transpired on these nightly jaunts was rife, but it was a discussion children were not allowed to hear. As with the Nurse Cadden affair Niamh found herself ordered out of earshot when Sergeant Doherty and Mrs. O'Casey were the subjects of conversation, but the children had their own theories.

"He takes her up to Phoenix Park and they do it in the holla," Rabba' O'Hare said, eyes popping with excitement.

"What do they do?" Niamh asked.

"She doesn't know." Rabba' gave her a pitying look and swept the other children with a colluding glance.

Niamh stood her ground. "So what do they do?" she asked again.

Rabba' smirked, a film of sweat forming on his upper lip where stray hairs sprouted. "He puts his thing in her thing," he guffawed, kicking at a tuft of grass. "It's what all mammies and daddies do to have a baby."

Niamh had no idea what he was talking about, but she pushed him hard on the chest. "You're a right omodon, so you are Rabba' O'Hare," she said.

*

All the while the people of the barracks talked and laughed and the kids, jeering and shouting, escorted the Morris Minor to the Cross Gate, Siobhan Doherty kept a lonely vigil. She did not up sticks and seek refuge from the humiliation and ridicule at her family's farm in County Tipperary. Instead, stupefied by the pain and shame of Tommy's public betrayal and seemingly unaware of her own courage, she sat each evening outside her flat rocking herself backwards and forwards, backwards and forwards, like a child seeking comfort.

Siobhan Doherty was not the only victim of the summer madness that gripped her husband. Her three young children endured taunts and jeers with bemusement and incomprehension. They knew their daddy had bought a car and that he had bought new clothes. They assumed they would have good times: that they would drive to the sea, have picnics, visit relatives down the country. Instead, their daddy went every evening, dressed in his silly clothes and collected Mrs. O'Casey and took her for a drive. And their mammy cried and cried. And some of the other children scoffed and spat at them and said things they didn't understand.

*

Private O'Casey was on duty at the Curragh when the romance started so everyone waited with bated breath for his return.

"There'll be skin and hair flying, so there will. He'll give Tommy a collop that will land him in the middle of next week and serve the bowsie right," Niamh overheard Mrs. Bolger tell her mammy, before she was ordered out, "away from where grownups are talking."

But Private O'Casey came home and still Tommy called for Francie and took her jaunting. And the cuckolded husband did nothing.

"It's because that one's insatiable. She's one of those maniacs: you know the ones who can't get enough of ... you know ... the other. He's probably delighted to have someone to help him out."

This time Niamh overheard the entire sentence, but she couldn't make head or tail of it.

Nearer the truth, as the adults knew, was that Sergeant Doherty outranked Private O'Casey

*

In the end it was Siobhan Doherty who took action and halted the affair, and a new song, sung to the air of *Frankie and Johnny*, entered the lexicon of the barracks, celebrating the fact that Siobhan grabbed hold of Francie's long tresses, dragged her the length and breadth of B Block, socked her one on the jaw, bowed deeply to the crowd of cheering women who witnessed the event before returning home to a trembling Tommy.

Niamh was left wondering why Mrs. Doherty had vented her spleen on Mrs. O'Casey and not her husband. She didn't frame her misgivings in these exact words, but she had a strong feeling that justice had not been done. Had her brothers, Daniel and

Paul, conspired to hurt her she would have tried to bash both their heads in.

*

Summer slipped slowly into autumn and then to winter. Children played conkers and when the ice and snow came, they stamped and buffed the hard-packed snow into a gigantic slide, a black ribbon that snaked from the corner of G Block to the end of F Block and which caught strangers who entered the barracks at night unawares, sending them slipping, sliding and sprawling along the shiny strip.

Adults settled into the gloomy months ahead and under cover of darkness the Dohertys and the O'Caseys left married quarters and the passion wagon was seen no more.

The Writers' Bar exuded comfort and intimacy, its entire ambiance radiating luxury and ease, but for those of mature years it was a snake pit of hazards. In the soft light Niamh was in danger of missing her step; the sofas threatened to swallow her entirely and she would need a ladder and a safety harness to mount one of the padded stools that encircled the crescent bar.

Spotting the possible difficulties W.B. had a discreet word with the waiter who ushered them, immediately, towards the Gallery Restaurant.

"I've ordered champagne, Aunty Niamh," he said, a smile lighting his handsome face, "Things went great in Cork so I thought we'd celebrate, if that's okay with you, ma'am?"

"Bubbly goes straight to my head," Niamh said with a giggle, "but I'm game for anything, provided you drop the ma'am. As this is the last time I shall see you I want to hear everything. Don't spare me; give me the full story."

Having waited for W.B.'s nod of assent the waiter poured two generous glasses of bubbly, put the bottle into an ice-bucket and withdrew.

"*Sláinte!*" Niamh said, "Here's mud in your eye kid — an appropriate mixture of vernaculars if I say so myself. Okay, my boy — shoot."

Between gulps of champagne W.B. blurted out his news. He had gone back to County Cork in search of his roots. Yes, he had told her that already, but the bit he hadn't mentioned was that his grandpa's name was Collins and that he was a descendent of Michael Collins. Yes, Michael Collins the republican leader. Michael Collins who had been responsible for organizing the War of Independence against the British. Michael Collins who'd been killed by fellow Irishmen in his home county — that Michael Collins.

Over the rim of her glass Niamh raised her eyebrow. "Not wanting to burst your bubble," she said, with a chuckle followed by the suggestion of a hiccup, "but almost everyone named Collins who comes from Cork claims to be related to the Big Fellow. If I were you I'd hold me horses; I wouldn't get excited without incontrovertible proof."

"You don't understand Aunty Niamh, I met the grandson of grandpa's brother and he says for sure we're related to Michael Collins."

"No doubt, but you could find a Collins under every stone in that part of Ireland all claiming to be related to the man himself."

"Brendan says that his grandfather has documentary evidence of the family connection and that he'll copy it and send it to me in the States."

"*Sláinte!*" Niamh said again, and this time her toast was accompanied by an audible burp.

As they ate their meal — grilled trout, saffron rice and a seasonal salad for Niamh, coddle for W.B. — he continued to recount his adventures.

"You know Michael Collins was born at Sam's Cross, well, so was grandpa. Brendan took me to the

Four Alls where Michael had a drink the night before he died and I had a pint of Clonakilty Wrastler, Michael's favourite beer. And we went to Woodfield and I saw the actual place where he was born — it's a stable now." He filled his mouth with a spoonful of stew and Niamh seized the moment.

"I've made good progress with *Ulysses*, I've reached the part where he is writing in archaic language and I wanted to ask you what Joyce was …"

"Cork is just full of monuments to my ancestor: there's one at Woodfield, two if you count the bust, one at The Valley of the Flowers where he was killed and there's a barracks named for him. There's a Collins Museum and a Collins Trail. Ain't that something?"

"There's a Collins' barracks in Dublin," said Niamh, taking a large gulp of champagne.

"No kidding! Maybe I could see it tomorrow before I head out."

*

"Do you think many men wank on a beach in full public view?" Niamh took another gulp of her drink before continuing and was gratified to note that at last she had W.B.'s undivided attention. "Of course, you may not be familiar with the term wank; I believe the American usage is jerk off."

W.B. placed his glass carefully on the table before answering. "I can't claim to be an expert on the subject, Aunty Niamh, but I guess from what I've seen on beaches it doesn't happen that often."

"Would you agree that Joyce was pushing the bounds of credibility when he had Bloom do just that on Sandymount Strand as he lusted after Gerty MacDowell? I'm interested in the male point of view."

"Do you reckon it's helpful to talk of a male point of view in relation to literature, Aunty Niamh?"

"Don't try to side-track me, my boy."

"Aunty Niamh, I think maybe you're doing a whole lot of side-tracking. I think maybe the Collins clan is not your favourite subject."

Niamh chewed slowly and swallowed a piece of fish. "It seems to me you've been bowled-over by what you've learnt about the Collins clan, but that's fine. It's the debasement of an heroic, intelligent, extraordinary man who gave his all for what he believed that I have difficulty with."

"But remembering the guy in no way diminishes him."

"Anyone genuinely interested in Irish history can put a bit of effort into reading about what he did, what he achieved and his legacy — although there's no doubt opinion differs on that — as you rightly said, his own country men killed him."

"Yes, but …

"I'm not so sure what's going on in Cork is for the glory of his memory — more like to make a few quid. Michael Collins would do somersaults and back flips in his grave if he knew that the whole of Cork had been turned into a theme park on his account and that's my last word on the matter."

The waiter, who had hovered discretely until Niamh stopped for breath, approached and removed their plates. He handed each a dessert menu and withdrew.

*

She was absolutely exhausted.

Served her right for wanting to swank at the Gresham.

She should have known that journeying from her hotel, traipsing around Rathmines and then back to the hotel was enough for one day.

W.B. was a fine young man, but he had the boundless energy and enthusiasm for which the Yanks were renowned and it could be very draining. Listening to him rave about the Collins of County Cork she'd almost expired with fatigue.

Her efforts to engage him with Joyce had come to nothing. He was too excited about coming back to his roots, about finding his ancestors.

*

As she settled herself to sleep she remembered, belatedly, the words of a Celtic blessing that would speed W.B. on his journey back to the land where his grandparents had sought a better life for themselves all those years ago. If any country had need of such a blessing it was Ireland: for centuries it had haemorrhaged its sons and daughters to the four corners of the globe.

Softly Niamh sang:
May the road rise with you.
May the wind be always at your back.
Until we meet again
I will hold you, in the hollow of my hand.

She awoke next morning overwhelmed by a sense of loss. Her sleep had not been disturbed by the usual black whirlpool, so she needed to look elsewhere for the cause. She lay in bed musing, until at last she located its source. She was sad because W.B. had left Dublin.

This idea was so preposterous that she allowed herself to prod, one by one, the tender spots of her individual sadnesses to see if they would bleat in pain, but the usual suspects failed to respond.

It was just too absurd to allow that the absence of a young man she had known for three days could make her feel bereft — it was too fanciful, too irrational.

"Get up you mad old hag," she told herself, "and continue your travels. You've only three and a half days left to complete your circuit."

*

She hesitated outside the hotel, unsure what to do. Because of her night on the tiles she hadn't given her route much thought, but she knew she didn't want to return to Rathmines that day. When she ventured there again, where the ghosts of her beginnings were as plentiful as fairies in the underworld (if her grandmother were to be believed) it would be for the last time so she would save it until her final day.

Today she would start at Sandymount and make her way along the seashore until she reached Killiney — the place she loved best in the entire world. She would cover the ground Stephen Dedalus had trekked in the opening scenes of *Ulysses*, but in reverse. Stephen's ramblings had taken him ever closer to the city. She was leaving it behind, retreating from its human clamour, opting for the tranquillity of long sandy beaches where she might close her eyes, imbibe the salty air, listen to the waves and the call of the gulls.

She would let her thoughts roam free.

Leave herself open to suggestion.

Try to make sense of her nightly terrors.

She knew it was possible to walk from Sandymount to Killiney if you were prepared to take your life in your hands and cross a few railway lines. But first she had to get herself to Sandymount. She crossed the road and headed for Booterstown Station. From there she would catch the DART to Sandymount and start her long trek.

*

During the twenty-three years she had lived in Dublin and on all subsequent visits, she had only once seen full tide at Sandymount. It was late at night and she and a friend were cycling home from Anglesea Tennis Club where they'd jived and bopped in the cramped clubhouse until they were drenched in sweat and their thickly lacquered *bouffant* hairstyles hung limp and bedraggled.

It was half past midnight and they should have headed straight home, but it was summer and the briny smell drew them to the strand. A full moon glowed on the black waves that battered the seawall and sent jets of lacy spray into the air.

Niamh and Deirdre leapt from their bicycles and stood, faces raised, arms outstretched, exulting in the chill of the water as it drenched their warm bodies.

"Hey young ones, here's young fellas," the shout was loud and harsh and was followed by braying laughter. Niamh and Deirdre dropped their arms and hurriedly retrieved their bikes. As they peddled quickly in the direction of home, the current Dublin courting cry followed them into the night.

"Get them off ya. Put them on your head; you're on next," the lads shouted, before breaking into hysterical laughter.

But Niamh had witnessed something spellbinding; something she'd never experienced on her many visits to Sandymount as a child. She had seen the vast expanse of Sandymount Strand filled by the sea: had heard the pounding of the waves as they rushed headlong towards the fragile boundary of the seawall, sending geysers of water flying towards the sky.

*

She alighted at Sandymount Station into the grey morning. She was nowhere near the sea so she asked a postman for directions. To make her way to the strand she would have to walk along Sandymount Avenue and take a right into Gilford Road.

Twenty minutes later she crossed Strand Road and headed out along the promenade towards the Martello Tower. Joggers raced past, taut muscles and, occasionally, generous wads of flab bulging in tight Lycra, wires trailing from iPods. If she lived to be a hundred (and who would want to do that) she would never understand the mania that had gripped recent generations to be entertained every second of the day, to be cut off from the sound of nature and of human activity, to choose instead the relentless beat of music piped directly into their skulls.

The strand was as she expected, vast and damp, dotted here and there with small pools of salt water and fading towards Howth into a misty horizon. Behind her, the giant chimneys of Pigeon House Power Station reached for the sky.

During the 1960s the residents of Sandymount had sent up an outraged howl as their precious view was threatened by these ugly monstrosities, but to no avail. The harbingers of progress had won the battle; the chimneys were built and the precious view was lost.

But the chimneys had become a well-loved landmark, apparently, and now it was the industrial historians who were sending up a howl of indignation because the ugly things were threatened with demolition. The site was destined for development as a high-density urban estate and the guardians of Ireland's industrial heritage were not happy.

"If you could only please half of the people quarter of the time sure wouldn't it be great?" the waiter in Niamh's hotel had remarked as he filled her in on the local argy-bargy. "My money's on the developers," he said, "they haven't lost a round in this city yet."

*

When the promenade and strand petered out she was forced onto the narrow path that ran alongside the beach road. Cars whooshed by every second, buffeting her in their slipstream, and she realized she had embarked on another hare-brained scheme. It would take her at least a week to make the journey along the coast to Killiney on foot. She was only on the outskirts of Sandymount and ahead she would have to negotiate Blackrock, Seapoint, Salthill, Dun Laoghaire, Sandycove and Dalkey. If she remembered correctly, to reach the strand at several of these destinations she would have to clamber up steep stairs, cross a railway bridge, descend a flight of steps and hurry through a smelly underpass before finally reaching her destination. And then she would have to retrace her steps before heading for the next port of call.

Just because Bloom had walked the feet off himself didn't mean she had to do the same. She had notched up another failure; but what matter, didn't her mother always say that there was no shame in failure; you just had to try again.

It was nearly time for coffee and she was close to the hotel so she would drop in there, refresh herself and do the sensible thing. She would return to Booterstown Station, buy a ticket for Killiney, catch a train and hop off at each station along the way.

*

She ordered a latte, sat on a comfortable leather seat in the foyer, took her book from her bag and started to read. She would have one last go at the section that had defeated her for two days. If she couldn't understand it this time she would move on.

She was two pages into it and still lost in a fug when she was interrupted.

"You're well into it then."

"Is that a statement or a question?" Niamh asked without taking her eyes off the book.

"I guess it could be either or both, begob. Take your pick."

"Well, it depends."

"On what, now, does it depend?"

Niamh glanced at the tiny man who was almost swallowed by the leather chair in which he sat. "It depends on whether you're asking if I've progressed well in my understanding of the book, or whether you mean I've read a large percentage of the pages."

"Sure if you've read as far as the book is opened then the latter goes without saying, but without discussing the matter with you I would have no idea about the former."

"I'll help you save your breath. I've read lots of pages, but I haven't a clue what's going on in this section."

"Sure you wouldn't be the first and no doubt you won't be the last. But if you hold on there a minute till I get a drink, I'll help you out."

As he walked towards the bar Niamh realized that she had seen him before: he was the man who had addressed her, rather cryptically, in Bewley's, on the day of her arrival. On closer examination it occurred to her that he bore an uncanny resemblance to Barry Fitzgerald, a pixie of a man who had played a roguish imp in many Hollywood films during the 1940s. There was, however, a major difference — this man's skin was dark as ebony and his greying black hair was curled tightly to his head — other than that, with his puckered face and deep set eyes, he was a dead ringer.

It was obvious that he had failed to recognize Niamh.

Despite the early hour, he ordered an Irish whiskey.

"Where were we?" he asked as he savoured a mouthful of the amber liquid, smacked, and then licked, his lips.

"I'm on the section that takes place in a maternity hospital, but once Joyce starts writing in Middle English and then keeps changing his style I'm lost: I may as well be looking into a bush."

"Don't feel too badly about it. Sure hasn't it taken dozens of academics years to decipher and, no doubt, they'll still be finding new meanings when you and I are both beneath the sod."

"If music be the food of love, play on," Shakespeare wrote. And if music were indeed the food of love the residents of Cathal Brugha Barracks were in danger of having a surfeit of it. Music resounded around every corner and during all waking hours.

The Army School of Music was based at Cathal Brugha Barracks. Boys of limited means from all over the country, who wanted to escape to the capital city and had a talent for music, joined at the age of fourteen and spent four years in Dublin. The *crème de le crème* of these musicians were chosen to play in The Number One Army Band whose rehearsal room was within yards of where Niamh lived. Five days a week, the brass and reed band rehearsed for their concerts. Consequently, the scores of *Showboat, Oklahoma, Carousel, South Pacific*, Bizet's *Carmen* and Gilbert and Sullivan's light operas soared from the Band Room, the rectangular redbrick building next to the Cross Gate. Many occupants of the nearby flats, unable to resist the pull of the music, opened their mouths and hearts and let rip, though Mrs. Mulholland was the only woman brave enough to attempt *Summertime*, Gershwin's sublime lullaby.

As her clear soprano soared higher and higher through the open window, her neighbours stopped working and listened in rapt silence until Mrs.

Murphy's cry of, "And then you woke up," brought them back to earth with a thump.

Niamh's mother could not match Mrs. Mulholland in the singing stakes, but she had a rare gift — any sentence uttered in her presence could prompt a song. A word would resonate and she was off. "Mammy, can I play with the girls?" might evoke, *Girls Were Made To Love and Kiss.* "Mammy, can I wear my black shoes?" and she'd launch into, *If I Were a Blackbird."* Although Niamh and her brothers longed for a simple answer to a simple question they valued their mother's singing: not only was it the musical score to their daily lives, it was also a good indicator of her moods.

Niamh took her mother's voice for granted, was sure it was sweet and tuneful, but Breda Mulholland put paid to that fancy. "Your mammy sounds like a crow," she told the amazed Niamh and received a punch in the gob for her trouble. But she had ruined the illusion. From then on Niamh listened to her mother's warbling with a critical ear and conceded that Breda had a point, but she would rather have jumped naked into the bed of stingers at the back of the flats than say it aloud.

*

Privileged as they were at having their own private band, there were also other musical riches available to the residents of the barracks. For those who favoured Radio Eireann over the B.B.C. programmes (and Niamh's parents did) an almost continuous loop of traditional Irish dance music and ballads was available throughout the day, with the occasional concert by Radio Eireann Symphony Orchestra thrown in.

For her mother, Walton's Music Programme, broadcast each Saturday afternoon, was a must. She would feed her family, wash the delph, seat herself in the comfortable chair by the fire, raise her feet onto a stool and, with closed eyes, give herself up to the fifteen minute programme, at the end of which Leo Maguire cried in ringing tones, "If you feel like singing, do sing an Irish song," and, taking his own advice, sang with gusto,

> "Land of Song sang the warrior Bard,
> Though all the world betray thee.
> One sword at least thy right shall guard,
> One faithful harp shall praise you."

Each Saturday Niamh's mother gave him lusty vocal support and her brothers marched round the table, imaginary swords clutched in their hands, mouthing their gibberish version of the stirring lyrics.

*

But never let it be said that the men of the barracks did nothing to contribute to its musical culture. It would have been a damn lie: a terrible calumny. For contribute they did, and gladly. But their contributions were sporadic and needed just the right amount of lubrication: too little and they would utter not a sound, too much and they would descend, into slurring incoherence.

Niamh's father, when called upon for his party-piece, harked back to the place of his birth. After the usual urgings, "Ah, go on, just one verse. Ah go on out of that, you know you want to, you know you do. Never let it be said that a Wexford man would refuse the challenge," he would clear his throat and, from shaky beginnings, fill the air with *Boolavogue,* the rousing rebel song of his county.

By the time he'd worked his way to the climax that paid homage to the brave Father Murphy, all the other adults had joined in and would end with a rousing cheer, while the children cringed with embarrassment.

Her father's best friend came from the west and *Galway Bay* was his usual offering.

"Throw yourself into it, Mr. O'Callaghan," Niamh's eldest brother had urged one Christmas night, and was sent to bed for his pains.

But the kids saved their loudest groan for Mr. Murphy, known as "the fella who would come for a wedding and stay for the christening". He hailed from Limerick and under the steely eye of their mothers, they were forced to sit quietly and endure an interminable dirge called *Down White's Lane.* The suspicion was that he made it up as he went along and the more fidgety the kids became, the longer he continued.

*

And then there were the kids.

They made their own music, though the music was an accompaniment to other activities rather than an end in itself.

As the girls skipped, so they sang. Politically ignorant, they nevertheless sang of the leading politicians of the day.

Someone produced a substantial length of rope; two strong girls volunteered as turners; the remainder formed a queue and they were ready for the off. The rope rose in a great arc, hit the road with a loud thwack, sending dust and gravel flying. The motion was repeated and the turners gradually picked up speed. The leader jumped in as the group sang,

"Vote, vote, vote for DeValera,
In walks Costello at the door hi, ho."
(The second skipper joined the first).
"Costello is the one with whom we'll have a bit of fun,
And we don't want Dev anymore, hi, ho."
(The first skipper jumped out).

And so the game continued until each girl had had her turn.

When they changed to culinary matters the turners upped the tempo and the skippers jumped in together, singing,

"Salt, mustard, vinegar, ginger, cayenne pepper.
Salt, mustard, vinegar, ginger, cayenne pepper.
Salt, mustard, vinegar, ginger, cayenne pepper."

Quicker and quicker they skipped until, one by one, they dropped out and only Breda Mulholland was left, jumping at a furious speed as the chant grew faster and faster still, and the turners worked with all their might. In the end Breda's energy and skill defeated them and they collapsed, sweating and exhausted.

They left romance until last, for two reasons. One: the routine was demanding and they had to build up to it. Two: they were shy.

The preliminary to this item involved a good deal of shoving, pushing and taunting.

"Niamh likes Paddy O'Brien."
"I do not, he's stupid."
"Peggy kissed Dermot Foster behind the handball alley."

"I did not. You're a liar, so you are."

"Kitty showed her knickers to Sean Foley, so she did."

Eventually, to the interminable verses of *I'll Tell Me Ma*, they jumped wildly over the twirling rope until, worn out, they trailed home and the rope disappeared, no one seemed to know where. But somehow it was found for the next session.

*

And then there were the boys

Until the advent of rock and roll the boys' musical efforts were meagre and had a military bent. There was the one about fighting and dying for Ireland to the shores of Tripoli and just one other. With hurleys placed on shoulders they arranged themselves in rows and marched from block to block, singing, robustly, of the testicular endowment (or lack of it) of Göring, Hitler, Himmler and Goebbels.

*

And for one magical summer it all came together. Mr. Reilly brought out his accordion, stood on his doorstep and played a rousing march. Before long a group of children had gathered. On that first evening the boys shoved, pushed and belted each other. The girls stood fiddling with their hair, giggling with excitement.

Mr. Reilly went straight into a jig and then a reel. Breda Mulholland, renowned for her skipping and dancing skills, gave a loud whoop, caught hold of Niamh's arm and spun her round and round. Soon everyone joined in and the clamour of music, laughter and squeals of excitement brought parents to their doors.

When Mr. Reilly changed the tempo and played a waltz, Mr. Murphy caught hold of Mrs. Murphy and twirled her round the road until she was dizzy and collapsed with exhaustion and delight.

All through the long hot summer, Mr. Reilly enchanted the people of the barracks. Each night his audience grew so they moved to the large square between G and F block where they danced lively reels, wild jigs and, especially for the grownups, romantic waltzes.

Those who didn't want to dance came to watch, claiming a front row seat on F Block. Mothers sat with sleeping babes on their laps with mesmerized toddlers close by. Men sipped beer. Mr. Reilly interspersed the jigs, reels and waltzes with rousing rebel songs and familiar ballads, and voices rose and soared to the starry skies as the good folk of the barracks opened their mouths and gave voice to all the yearning and longing of their bruised hearts.

"Elizabeth Carroll, at your service," said Barry Fitzgerald's look-a-like, offering Niamh a small hand, dark as a nut and smooth as velvet. She grinned wickedly at Niamh's look of surprise. "Don't let it worry you; most people make the same mistake. Even this late in the evolutionary process if you don't adhere to accepted notions of femininity people assume you're either a man or queer, or both."

"Is that a Kerry accent?" Niamh asked. "I'm sorry; I've lived away a long time."

"And the nuances of culchie accents are a bit beyond you, now? Arrah, sure it is indeed, and I suppose you're wondering how an oul' one like me has a Kerry accent?"

"You were going to explain *Ulysses* to me," Niamh said.

"In so far as Joyce's masterpiece can be explained, I'll do my best. Where do you want to start?"

"To be honest I've had difficulty throughout, but the episode about the maternity hospital has me completely flummoxed."

"Ah, sure that's where Bloom and Stephen come together, and it's an episode that particularly excites linguists because doesn't Joyce pull off an amazing feat — within this one chapter he reproduces each phase in the development of the English language.

How about that then?" Elizabeth paused, took a gulp of whiskey and let the import of her words sink in.

"I have to admit I didn't get that."

"Sure, and why would you unless you'd had a misspent maturity reading Joyce and his critics."

*

At half-past-twelve, at Elizabeth's suggestion, they moved to the dining room and ordered lunch. Niamh ordered seafood pasta, garlic bread and a green salad. Elizabeth opted for coddle.

Niamh waited until her hunger had been satisfied before opening the discussion once again. "I hesitate to say this, but the most accessible and interesting aspect of this chapter for me is the vivid depiction of childbirth and the knowledge of obstetrics it displays."

"Sure why would you not want to say what you think? You've taken from the book what's most relevant to you and what's wrong with that?"

"But surely the whole purpose of reading fiction is to be taken beyond yourself, to broaden your understanding of the world, to grapple with unfamiliar ideas?"

"You don't half like to give yourself a hard time."

Elizabeth explained to Niamh that she read better than she realized, her feminine instincts had not failed her. The chapter she was having difficulty with was structurally complex: as it mirrors the development of the English language it also mirrors the entire process from conception to birth. Three sections divide into nine subsections that represent the trimesters and months of gestation.

"How about that then?" she asked. "Although," she added, "not all critics agree on this."

*

After coffee they decided, in order to prevent themselves seizing up entirely, that exercise was called for so they went for a walk by the sea.

The sun had won the battle and the early-morning mist had taken itself off in a huff, gifting a shimmering warm afternoon to those fortunate enough to be out and about. The tide retreated slowly and the gentle waves sparkled and shone in the bright light.

As they strolled along in silence, Elizabeth lit a slim cigar, drew deeply, and exhaled with satisfaction.

"It's great to be home on afternoons like this," Niamh said.

"Isn't that an interesting use of the word home?" Elizabeth replied.

"How's that?"

"You said earlier that you've been away from Ireland a long time, yet you still call the place home.

"Habit," Niamh said.

"May I venture to suggest it's a habit you should have abandoned a long time ago?"

*

A dog, its fur matted and thick with salt water, bounded across the strand towards them, skidded to a halt, circled them madly and raced off in response to its owner's whistle.

"Were you born in Kerry?" Niamh asked.

Despite her diminutive size Elizabeth's laugh was loud and hearty. "Are you joking me?" she said, "Things like me weren't even heard of in Kerry seventy years ago, let alone born there."

"If you don't mind me asking, how did you land up in that remote spot?"

Elizabeth didn't mind Niamh asking at all, and to be sure it was very simple. She'd been born and brought up in Jamaica, had emigrated with her parents to England, attended university where she'd developed an interest in postcolonial studies years before that discipline existed. She had pursued her own line of research, discovered that some of her ancestors had been sent as slaves from Ireland to the West Indies, had secured tenure at Trinity and, when circumstances allowed, she went to live in Kerry because that's where her Irish relatives had been dragged from, some time in the seventeenth century.

"How about that then?"

*

"You might find the next episode of *Ulysses* the most challenging yet," Elizabeth said as they continued along the beach. "Although the action takes place within a short time-frame it's the longest in the novel and moves backwards and forwards between realism and a series of hallucinations."

"What's the point of that?"

"Sure there are probably as many theories as there are critics, but to my way of thinking, by embracing the surreal the author claims the freedom to break taboos and push at boundaries. It's a useful device to employ when exploring Bloom's basest instincts and the reality of his marriage. And Joyce really seems to enjoy letting go of the reins of reality. Doesn't he have a whale of a time?"

"I'm wondering if I have the stamina for it," Niamh said.

"Why did you choose to read it on holiday?"

Niamh opened her mouth to explain and closed it again. She thought for a little while longer and then asked Elizabeth if she would mind if they rested on the large rocks by the sea wall. They sat in silence, looking at the lapping waves.

"Don't feel you have to answer," Elizabeth said.

Niamh explained that she had first encountered the book in her final year at the University of Birmingham, had considered taking the Joyce option under the tutelage of David Lodge, had taken one look at *Ulysses*, decided she was on to a sticky wicket, and changed her mind. As a mature student with three children to look after and a home to run, she was already hanging on by the skin of her teeth and needed the easiest options possible. But she had bought the book and it had sat in her bookcase in silent rebuke for many years until, three years previously, she had moved it to her bedside table. During the past three years it had moved from the table to the bookcase several times, having been dipped into and abandoned again and again. To compensate for her failure to grasp the nettle and to prepare herself for the monumental task, she had reread *Dubliners* and *A Portrait of the Artist* twice, had read some biographical stuff on the web, but that hadn't helped at all.

"But sure why do you feel compelled to read it?" Elizabeth ventured as Niamh stopped for breath.

"Because it is an avowed masterpiece by a fellow jackeen."

"If that's your criteria you'll never have time for sleep; you'd have to read not just Joyce but Shaw,

Wilde, Yeats, O'Casey, Behan, Beckett, Evan Boland and god knows how many others."

"I think it's the central action of *Ulysses* that is so appealing to a Dubliner who is an emigrant." Niamh looked across the bay and caught a glimpse of the Holyhead ferry making its way out to sea. "What Joyce has Bloom do is the stuff of every exile's dreams. Leopold walks his city during the course of one day, meeting people who know him and his family well, or slightly, or by hearsay, and it is this knowing that makes his life meaningful, that affirms who he is, acknowledges his significance as a human being."

"Now, I don't know that that was Joyce's intention," Elizabeth interrupted. "Didn't he set out to show how alienated his two main characters were in their own city?"

"Is the author's intention that significant? It seems to me that whether Bloom is liked or not by his fellow Dubliners is not the most important thing. The important thing is that he is among people who are aware of his history — a very appealing notion for the emigrant who, by necessity, lives among strangers." Niamh paused and then continued. "Joyce lived outside Ireland for most of his life, so he had first-hand knowledge of this experience."

She looked across the bay and saw the ferry disappear around the headland.

"I think it's a measure of the power of this notion that makes so many people talk about the book — even those who haven't read it know about Bloom's wanderings — and it's a measure of the difficulty of the book that makes so many people abandon it."

"May I venture a modest proposal?" Elizabeth asked. "You see, there are just two ways to approach *Ulysses* ..."

"And they are?"

"You can go the academic route and read it with the critics to hand. Only choose this method if you are prepared to make it your life's work."

"It's a bit late for that," Niamh said. "My life's work is almost behind me."

"Sure then you have only one option — read the bloody thing. Go along for the ride and to hell with comprehension."

*

Elizabeth and Niamh walked slowly back to the hotel. The evening traffic had built up at a terrifying rate and, foolishly, they attempted to cross the road beyond the pedestrian crossing and almost came a cropper.

"I could murder a drink after that," Elizabeth said, as they entered the foyer. "I'm going to meet Hubert in the bar, do you want to come?"

Niamh declined. She was tired, and besides, one of her precious days had melted away. She had made no further progress in her own personal odyssey around Dublin and she was running out of time. But at least she could spend the remainder of the day tackling the second strand of her plan. She would crash out on the bed and read Joyce. But before she took her departure she had one last question for the tiny academic.

"Why do you think Joyce wrote a book that was so difficult comparatively few people would actually read it in its entirety?"

Elizabeth smiled. "Sure that's simple," she said, and paused for effect. "Joyce wrote *Ulysses* because he could."

"That's it?"

"Yes, it's as simple and as complicated as that. He wrote *Ulysses* because he had the genius to do it — the intelligence, knowledge, wit, talent, desire and compulsion. How about that then?"

*

Niamh lay on her bed, following Elizabeth's diktat. She was reading quickly skimming the pages trying to read for sensation rather than meaning though she wasn't sure she knew how to do that but she kept going inhaling imagery recoiling at grotesquery marvelling at unusual compounds amazed at the spite and hate that bounced off the pages the venomous wit the exposition of the baseness and resilience of man and woman.

The intelligence, knowledge, wit, talent that Elizabeth had mentioned were all there for anyone to see. But reading without comprehension was a tiring business, and, although she fought valiantly against its pull, the vortex of her own dream world dragged her into its swirling mass.

The DART chugged along on its way to Blackrock. The tide was far out and the morning was grey and misty, but the forecast was good, so no worry on that score.

She had awoken at six o'clock, drained and exhausted from battling her nightly demons, but, undeterred, she got stuck into the book again, skimming along, flying through it she was. Not a clue what was going on except that Bloom was, by turns, humiliated and jubilated — if there was such a word and if there wasn't then there should be. Read fifty pages and then up and showered; ate a hearty breakfast and here she was at last on her coastal trip. She would get off at the next stop, have a little stroll on the beach, back onto the next train and keep repeating the process until she reached Killiney; lunch at the hotel, some more reading and then the return journey.

Great.

No complaints.

> How is you oul one?
> Game Ball.
> Out in the back yard.
> Playing ball.
> Who does she play for?
> Donegal.

> What is the score?
> Three all.

Absolutely.
It was good to be alive
She was having a ball.

*

After dinner the previous night, for the first time since her arrival, she had checked her emails and was delighted to have received one from W.B. His grandma was doing fine and sure was pleased with the news of his journey to Cork and with the photographs he'd taken, especially of Yeats' Garden. His grandma would sure like Niamh to come visit. So if she'd like a trip to New York just let him know. And he hadn't forgotten about Joyce. As soon as he had time he would dig out his old essays and send her copies.

She had also received an email from Jessica who was in America, travelling coast to coast. No word from either Tim or Harry. Only to be expected what with Tim exploring the Amazon, and Harry travelling in Africa.

Niamh didn't think her enthusiasm for Joyce went as far as reading undergraduate essays, but she was touched by W.B.'s generosity. Perhaps the book was a good luck talisman after all. It certainly attracted attention and everyone had something to say about it. Whether any of it was accurate was another matter. Probably the toss could be argued either way, and it would be difficult to be proven right or wrong. Maybe that's what Joyce intended. Maybe he wanted to write a book that would keep the literary world in a constant state of ferment. Perhaps it was his revenge on the

English for eight hundred years of colonization. He had written a book in the conquerors' language that they would spend eight hundred years interrogating.

Fair play to him.

There are more ways than one.

*

She was the only soul on Blackrock Strand. She was glad the tide was a good way out, otherwise she would have had to clamber over the great rocks and she wasn't up to that anymore.

She had never really felt safe at Blackrock. Unlike Sandymount, where water deep enough to swim was as rare as a celibate priest, the tide always seemed to be splashing over the rocks and if you jumped into the sea you were in danger of being in above your head and maybe drowning. Her feelings of anxiety had been heightened by one of Daniel's stories. "Balor is the king of demons," he had told her. "His demons live at the bottom of the sea where it's really dark. They're called Fomoire. They are huge lumps of black flesh with enormous mouths." Daniel's eyes bulged and he opened his mouth wide. He hooked two fingers at each side of his mouth, pulling it wider still. Hunkering down, he put his face next to Niamh's. "They have no arms or legs. They come to places where there are big rocks so that they can slither onto them in the dark and look for people to eat. That's why they like Blackrock." He ended his tale with a roar that sent Niamh scampering down the beach towards her mother.

As a young woman, after work on hot summer evenings, she and a friend would catch a bus from O'Connell Street to Blackrock and, if the tide was clear of the rocks, they would splash about in the cool green water (making sure they left before dark) eyeing the talent and, like every generation of teenagers before and since, giggled compulsively and uproariously at nothing at all. Lately she was given to wondering whether the ear-splitting shrieks of young women on buses or in the street were a mechanism for blocking out the terror of the reality they were about to inherit.

But sod them.

It wasn't her concern anymore.

Let them, with their skimpy dresses and mile-high heels see if they could make a better fist of things.

*

Back on the train, off again at Seapoint Station that had been built, Elizabeth had told her, in 1862. Its Martello Tower, built in 1804, had been given to the Genealogical Society of Ireland by Dublin Corporation about ten years previously for use as its headquarters and had been tastefully refurbished. Wasn't that great? With millions of Irish and their descendants all over the world keen to dig for their roots the Society grew busier every year. It was amazing what you could make a living from these days. She must send W.B. an email and tell him about it.

Niamh had always preferred the beach at Seapoint to that of Blackrock. She was never sure, she had told her father (unwisely as it turned out), how deep the water would be in Blackrock and received a lecture on the movement of the tides and on how to check them. She simply needed to read the times in the daily newspaper where they were printed for any omodon to see. She lived in a coastal city and had a duty to avail herself of this information before heading off and risking her life by attempting to swim in deep water when her swimming wasn't up to much and maybe putting some poor eejit in mortal danger when he tried out of the goodness of his heart to rescue her.

While she had continued to live in Ireland she had ignored this paternal advice. The sea simply was. It was the background to her growing up, something to be taken for granted like her mammy and daddy, her brothers — a natural part of her life. However, if she were abroad and by the sea, she remembered her father's words and approached the water with due caution, except once, when she was in Corfu and had believed what the thick ignorant guide had told her about there being no shelf on the beach and had nearly drowned as a result.

*

"Hey, missus, can you give us five euros?" one of four boys, about twelve years old she would guess although youngsters today seemed so big that she could be wildly wrong and they might be only six or seven, called to her. She ignored him.

"Hey, you, are you deaf? Can you give us five euros?"

Niamh continued to ignore the lads, but she increased her pace and headed towards a man who was walking his dog.

"Hey, you, you silly oul' bag, give us five euros." This time they had all shouted in unison and sang a rhyme.

"The hoor in the sewer.
The prick with the stick,
The tart with the cart,

The hag with the bag."

Niamh began to tremble. She was scared and who wouldn't be with what you read in the papers these days and saw on the telly every night that's if you looked at telly and you'd want to be mad for it was all rubbish but she was more angry than scared how dare the little brats talk to a woman of her years like that or a woman of any years come to that there was no rearing in the children today and why weren't they at school?

She continued walking in the direction of the man with the dog but didn't seem to be making any headway it wasn't that he was walking away from her he was walking in her direction but she could hear feet pounding on the strand behind her and they were getting closer and closer.

She was shoulder-barged stumbled put her hands out to break her fall managed to keep her feet was pushed on the rump landed on the wet sand and as she was falling her bag was pulled from her grasp.

"The hoor in the sewer,
The prick with the stick,
The tart with the cart,
The hag without the bag."

She was on her hands and knees on the strand the dog galloped up and licked her face and the man gave chase as the four lads ran off throwing the contents from her bag which blew in the wind towards the water and when they found what they wanted the bag was kicked like a football but it didn't travel just hit the sand with a thud because the heavy book was still in it.

The man rescued the bag and walked towards her.

"Scarlet fever, 1, 2, 3,
Scarlet fever, you and me.
Scarlet fever, 4, 5, 6,
Scarlet fever, fun and tricks."

Niamh's singing was brought to an abrupt halt by a stinging clip round the ear.

"Whist your nonsense and go and find your brother."

Niamh ran outside to do her mother's bidding and was stopped in her tracks by the unnatural hush which shrouded the wide road between A and B Blocks: the usual groups of shouting, running, screaming children were absent. Here and there a lone child hurried along, keen to be in out of the unnatural quiet. Mrs. Finnegan, renowned for her ability to blather endlessly about absolutely nothing, stopped briefly for a cursory exchange with Mrs. Dwyer before hastening indoors. The air was clouded with unease and a sense of dread.

"Scarlet fever 1. 2. 3.
Scarlet fever, you and me,
Scarlet fever, 4, 5, 6,
Scarlet fever fun and tricks."

"Shut up." Niamh looked upwards into the angry face of her big brother who was hanging over the railings of the veranda. "Shut up," he said again, "scarlet fever is horrible: it makes people die."

*

Scarlet fever.

The words were repeated again and again and with every utterance fear grew — a palpable presence sneaking around every corner, stealing into every home. Children, who were used to being shooed out of doors from under their parents' feet, were now kept close; encouraged to stay inside and make paper hats, play jackstones and push ha'penny. Some fathers parted with their precious decks of cards and games of Snap, Beggar-my-neighbour, Twenty-ones, Big Don and Little Don were played again and again with lollipop sticks used as stakes. Girls dressed in their mothers' old clothes, hobbled round in high-heeled shoes. Boys, for the most part opted out of this game: those who opted in were called sissy.

Children were scrutinized by anxious parents, once, twice, three times a day, for the tell-tale signs of the disease — swollen tonsils, a bright red skin rash and strawberry tongue. Before the widespread use of penicillin any combination of these symptoms gave rise to panic.

The spooky outdoor silence was broken frequently by the harsh bell of an ambulance as it raced into married quarters and removed yet another child from terrified parents. Most of these children were returned within a few weeks, pale and wan, many with peeling skin. Most made a full recovery.

The Byrne and the Hogan families were the unlucky ones: each suffered the agony of bereavement. Cathleen Byrne aged eight and Michael Hogan aged seven returned home briefly, but left a few days later for their last resting place in Mount Jerome Cemetery.

During those few days the children of the barracks were encouraged to view the bodies of their young friends. The prospect of making this visit filled Niamh with dread, but she knew, short of falling ill herself, there was no escaping her duty.

"It's a mark of respect to the family," her mother had told her when Niamh begged to be let off, "and besides you'll be in the presence of a saint. Isn't every child innocent and without sin, so anything you pray for will be granted. And the prayers of one child are worth more than those of ten adults, so out you go and do as you're told."

Her mother had imparted more information then Niamh could assimilate and she thought some of it conflicted with what Sister Scholastica had said about children and sin, but it was all too confusing and she wasn't sure why she had to go but she knew, without a shadow of a doubt, go she must.

She went to Cathleen Byrne's home, circling D Block several times, waiting for the queue of subdued children to disappear. Although she was scared of what she had to do, she didn't want to see the body of her dead friend in the company of others.

At last the queue had gone and Niamh approached the front door of the Byrne's flat, knocked and waited. Her heart was pounding. Its steady rhythm echoing in her ears drowned out the sound of the door opening.

"Yes, Niamh?" Mrs. Byrne was tall and thin. Her thick black hair was pulled into a bun that sat atop her head, making her taller still. She wore a black blouse and black skirt. Her bruised eyes were the only hint of colour; they stood out like ripe plums in her ashen face.

"Can I say a prayer for Cathleen, Mrs. Byrne?"

"Come in." Mrs. Byrne sounded as though she was choking.

Living as she did with her mammy, daddy, brothers, dog, cat and budgie, Niamh was used to a good deal of background noise, a home that was rarely silent. As she followed Mrs. Byrne into the sparsely furnished bedroom where Cathleen's body was laid out, it was the ghostly silence that struck her most forcibly. There was no voice talking, no music from the radio, no sound of children playing or squabbling — just an unearthly hush.

Mrs. Byrne left the room and Niamh was alone. She averted her eyes; unable to look at what lay on the bed. She knelt as far as possible from the cold waxen shell of her friend and started to pray.

"Dear Mother of God," she pleaded, "please let Cathleen live in a part of heaven where there are lots of children making lots of noise. And please can she have a skipping rope because she loved skipping. Amen."

A few minutes later Cathleen's mother opened the front door and Niamh escaped into the fresh air. Belatedly remembering her manners, she turned to say good-bye. Mrs. Byrne was standing on the doorstep, her shoulders stooped, tears streaming from her eyes, her face suffused with a look of longing and sadness that Niamh would never forget and which forced her to make a decision.

She would not go and pray by Michael Hogan's remains.

She would pray for him in her own room.
And she would lie to her mother if need be.

*

As the children and parents of Cathal Brugha Barracks worried and fretted and fought to stay well and alive, the government of Ireland and the Catholic Church were locked in a battle to determine who controlled the nation.

The 1947 Health Act was introduced by the *Fianna Fáil* government (led by DeValera) Part III of which provided for the Mother and Child Scheme. But before the government could implement the legislation it was ousted from office. The new inter-party government, led by Costello, held fire on the scheme until 1950 when Dr. Noel Browne, Minister for Health, proposed introducing a bill which would provide free maternity care for all mothers and free healthcare for all children up to the age of sixteen, regardless of income.

Although some members of the catholic hierarchy saw some merit in the proposals, the old guard, under the auspices of Archbishop McQuaid, let rip. The good Archbishop insisted that it was the exclusive right of all parents to provide healthcare for their children. It didn't seem to dawn on McQuaid that some families might not be able to afford such care.

But allow the archbishop the benefit of the doubt. Given the line of work he was in, he probably expected the lord would provide; after all, the lord had made ample provision for him and his cronies.

But on the other hand and to be fair, there was ample evidence that the lord frequently failed to provide and that mothers and children died as a result of this failure.

But looking at it from the point of view of the archbishop, it was probably more important that legislation which could pave the way for birth control and abortion be stopped than that mothers and babies receive vital medical care.

In the heel of the hunt, and at the end of the day, the church — aided and abetted by doctors who feared a loss of income — won the battle. Although the law changed, gradually, in the interim, scores of mothers and their children suffered as a result of the intervention of the church, and Nurse Cadden was ensured a regular supply of patients and the kids in the barracks, with uncanny insight, sang their skipping rhyme,

"Vote, vote, vote for DeValera,
In walks Costello at the door, hi, ho.
Costello is the one with whom we'll have a bit of fun,
And we don't want Dev anymore hi, ho,"

alternating the names because, as Niamh's father said, not caring if his children heard, "It doesn't matter a tinker's cus who sits in the *Taoisach's* chair in the Dail because the elected representatives of the people willingly and cravenly abdicate their power to the representatives of the church and until that stops this country will remain in the dark ages."

"Dear god, don't blaspheme," her mother said.

But the kids had the last word.

"Vote, vote, vote for Costello,
In walks Dev at the door, hi, ho.
Dev is the one with whom we'll have a bit of fun,
And we don't want Costello anymore hi, ho."

Having licked Niamh's face Roxy the dog chased after the four lads, thinking to join in their game. He threw himself at each item flung from her bag, sniffed it, slobbered over it and then raced off once again in hot pursuit of his young playmates. In the meantime, Willie Brown, all six feet four of him, picked her up off the wet sand as though she were a rag doll, and placed her carefully on a flat rock, intending to phone for an ambulance. But Niamh had found sufficient strength to dissuade him. She simply needed a taxi to her hotel and she could manage from there.

*

She sat in bed, propped comfortably against the pillows that the receptionist had arranged. Although inwardly trembling and shaking from her ordeal, she would not show her fear. She insisted she was all right; none the worse for wear. But the hotel management were not convinced. The doctor had to be sent for, meals would be served in her room (at no extra charge) and she must rest. She had suffered a shock that would unnerve a person half her age and she must do as advised.

Niamh had balked at the reference to her age. She had not survived the slings and arrows of outrageous fortune this long by being a wimp. As soon as a few wrinkles and a couple of strands of grey hair began to show, you were treated like a doddering twit, a helpless fool.

So here she was three hours later: the doctor had visited and prescribed rest and a light sleeping pill; a young garda had arrived and had taken a statement as her walkie-talkie, crackling and spluttering, leapt into intermittent life. The Spanish waitress with perfect English and a gentle manner, had brought her lemon sole, potatoes, peas and carrots, followed by gooseberry tart and cream, coffee and mints.

The little gurriers on the beach had not bothered with her credit cards or mobile phone. They had been after cash so had taken her purse. Thankfully, *Ulysses* had escaped unscathed. The only problem was that the book was so thick and heavy that her wrists ached from holding it in place so she turned on the telly for a little distraction and, very quickly, turned it off again. Chaos reigned on every front: bloody wars were being fought all over the place; suicide bombers, created in ever-greater numbers by the mindless activities of countries that should know better, were wreaking savage havoc; an unregulated financial world was in freefall — the consequences of all of this were too awful to contemplate.

She returned to reading her book, but with little enthusiasm. The catechism technique chosen by Joyce — formal question followed by specific answer — for this episode was mind-blowingly dull. There was no doubting the intelligence of the author — Joyce made sure of that — he covered a stupendously wide range of subjects and used a stupendously wide-ranging vocabulary, but it was the stupendous cleverness of it all that got on her tits (to use a

Brummie expression). However, determined to complete the book while in Dublin, she pressed on.

Bloom and Stephen were, apparently, urinating when blessed relief arrived.

"Come in," Niamh called in response to the knock on her door and was delighted when Barry Fitzgerald's look-a-like entered the room.

"I heard about your mishap and thought a drop of the hard stuff might do you good," Elizabeth said, waving a bottle of whiskey above her head as she tottered towards the bed.

Niamh tried to decline this generous offer, muttering about sleeping pills, but the inebriated academic would have none of it.

"You're only old once," she said, "and not for long." With a knowing wink she continued. "Put down that feckin' book out of that, give us a glass and have a slurp of the *uisce baithe* for god's sake."

*

The sun set in a blaze of orange, crimson and gold that lanced a corner of the room with blinding rays of light. The glorious palette gradually subsided into grey and then to black, dotted here and there by the silver of twinkling stars, but the occupants of the room were unaware of nature's brilliant display.

Niamh's head was thrown back against the pillow, her mouth open as she breathed deeply. The empty glass had dropped from Elizabeth's hand and she had fallen forward from the bedside chair, her head resting on the duvet, her snores coming in snorts and whistles.

A group of young men and women made their way noisily along the corridor, intent on waking any spoilsports who had already taken to their beds. The sound of their hysterical laughter and bellicose shouts caused Elizabeth to wake.

"That was Joyce's favourite episode," she declaimed into the dark room. When no response was forthcoming, she tried again. "I said it was his favourite episode," she shouted.

Niamh stirred. "Oooh! Oooh!" she moaned. "There's a Bangra drummer inside me head. Oh, my god!"

"I think I've lost me sight," Elizabeth said, "I can't see a thing."

"Don't you dare switch on a light, do you hear me?" Niamh whispered.

"What did you say? I've gone deaf as well as blind. Maybe it's time I gave up the drink."

*

They sipped scalding coffee and iced water intermittently. The drinks had been delivered to the room by a handsome Italian waiter, along with a ham salad sandwich for Elizabeth and tuna and mayonnaise for Niamh.

"I never drink, well apart from a glass of wine with my dinner, and now I know why."

"Sure anyone who's tired of drinking is tired of life, to paraphrase Johnson," Elizabeth said, 'for there is in drink all that life has to offer."

"That's nonsense."

"Spoken like a true Pioneer — the most boring tossers in the human race."

Niamh finished her sandwich, struggled from the bed and went into the bathroom where she relieved herself, washed her hands (careful not to look in the mirror) and returned to the bedroom. The sight of Elizabeth's profile stopped her in her tracks. All life and animation had leaked from the tiny woman's face. When speaking and laughing her flesh puckered into taut folds that kept the years at bay; at rest the flesh lost its elasticity, sagged and drooped.

*

Niamh climbed into bed and settled herself comfortably. A glance at the clock told her that it was very late. If she didn't get to sleep soon she would waste more precious time tomorrow. Both her reading and rambling schedules were way off course.

"You must be exhausted," she said.

"Sure why would I be exhausted, I do nothing."

"I thought you said you'd come to Dublin to attend a conference."

"Sure what does that mean, except that I've nothing better to do with my time than listen to people who love the sound of their own voices ramble on about the significance of the comma in the work of Henry James?"

"They must have something more interesting to say than that."

"When you've been listening to them for as long as I have everything they say sounds like irrelevant tripe. I mean what difference does it make to the world how James punctuated his work?"

"Would you like to tag along with me on my rambles to-morrow? Of course we'll have to stay sober."

"Drink is the scourge of this nation, so it is. I hate it. I just hate the damn thing; it's a curse." Niamh's mother moved round the kitchen, slowly and wearily.

Niamh and her brothers sat in silence, fearful of their mother's anger. During their short lives they had occasionally overheard heated exchanges between their parents that included the phrases, "dirty rotten drink", "waste of money", "a man needs an outlet", but their father had been working nights and had not, for some time, stumbled round the house or knocked against the furniture as he struggled to find the lavatory in the middle of the night, so it was difficult to identify the target of their mother's fury.

"He's a bowsie, that's what he is: a dirty rotten black-guard. I don't know why the lord can take innocent children, but allow the likes of that animal to live."

Tears started in Niamh's eyes, overflowed and streamed down her face. Underneath the table, Jack aimed a warning kick that connected with her ankle and made matters worse.

"My daddy's not a bowsie," she sobbed, "I want my daddy."

Her mother gave a start and looked at Niamh in surprise. She shook her head and with a great effort focused on her daughter. "No one's talking about your daddy," she said, "finish your breakfast and go out and play."

*

The men of Cathal Brugha Barracks were no better or worse than the population at large when it came to quaffing the hard stuff, but access to drink was made easy because of the close proximity of the mess for both corporals and sergeants where drink could be had cheaply and away from the watchful eyes of women.

In a community where families were large and incomes low the breadwinner's attitude to drink could mean the difference between having enough to eat and going hungry.

But nothing is as simple as it may seem. Most of the people who lived in the barracks were practising catholics which meant the use of contraception was not an option (had it been available) so, frequently, the choice had to be made — whether to encourage your man to stay home, with the attendant temptations, or send him off to have a few drinks in the hope that his ardour might be dampened or, failing that, you might get away with feigning sleep on his return.

Teetotallers were a rare breed. It was a brave man who would refuse a drink when it was alcohol that oiled the wheels of male camaraderie: made you one of the lads, a man who was boss in his own home. And, of course, many men drank in moderation, some even enjoying the occasional night out with their wives in civvy-street. But many families were forced to endure the hardship of harbouring a heavy drinker. If they were lucky this meant going short of food, shoes and other basic necessities: if they were unlucky it meant a life lived in fear and dread, listening for shuffling footsteps and suffering the beatings and kickings which invariably followed daddy's homecoming.

*

With the inevitable growth of their family the O'Riordans were offered one of the few three-bedroom flats available in married-quarters, situated on the ground floor of the block they lived in. Because the flat was said to be haunted there was no great demand for it and, although Niamh's mother believed in such phenomenon, she was so desperate to move from their present home she did not allow her fear to deter her. Instead, before making a final decision on whether to accept the flat she bribed her two older sons with a promise of their own room and sent them to spend a night there. When they failed to report any unusual noises or spiritual manifestations, she immediately moved her family into their new home.

Mrs. O'Riordan's urge to move was not prompted only by the desire for more space: relations between herself and her immediate neighbours had deteriorated to such an extent that she felt the move was imperative for the safety of her children.

Niamh's mother had been pleased when Sergeant McGillicuddy took up residence next door with his wife and two daughters. He was known as a quiet man and a teetotaller and, while these attributes did not recommend him to his military colleagues, they appealed to Mrs. O'Riordan.

Unfortunately, her pleasure was short-lived. The sergeant was a tall taciturn man, his two young daughters pale and withdrawn, his wife a volatile virago. On good days Mrs. McGillicuddy was jovial, good-humoured, generous. On her bad days she was a dark menacing force who felt the people, regardless of age, who inhabited her world were out to get her.

"Mrs. McGillicuddy is like The Morrigú, Queen of Battle, who screams at everyone and tears their arms and legs off," Daniel told his mother and received a clip round the ear for his pains. Worse still, he was warned that if he didn't shut his senseless blather his book of Irish mythology would end up in the fire.

In more enlightened times it would have been acknowledged that the poor woman was suffering from a serious illness; in 1950s Ireland she was seen as an evil manipulative harridan.

For one long, exhausting, horrifying summer every time Mrs. McGillcuddy encountered Niamh and her brothers (she passed their flat each time she left home so this was a frequent occurrence) she shouted, spat and snarled, her face distorted with fury.

"Kiss me arse," she bawled at Niamh's father as he stood on the veranda, resplendent in his pristine uniform: buttons, boots and leggings polished to a high shine, smoking his pipe before heading off for his shift at Leinster House.

Niamh watched fearfully from the doorway. Apart from her mammy she'd never heard anyone raise a voice to her father. She saw him stiffen in surprise. He took a long drag on his pipe, removed it from his mouth, banged the bowl on the railings. He looked at Mrs. McGillicuddy.

"I'd rather kiss it than your face, ma'am," he said. He turned away from the crazed woman, caught hold of the handlebars of his bicycle and wheeled it along the veranda.

*

Mrs. McGillicuddy's revenge was swift and violent.

Niamh stood, holding her mammy's bicycle outside Breda Mulholland's door, waiting for her friend so that they could go for an evening spin around Rathmines.

"Run, Niamh, run." Fear distorted her mother's voice and it took several vital seconds before she recognized it. As she turned she saw her raging neighbour bearing down on her.

"Run, Niamh, run. Drop the bike. Run." Her mother's voice was closer, but Mrs. McGillicuddy was upon her, grabbing the handlebars. The demented woman and Niamh engaged in a frantic dance round and round the bike as neighbours, frozen with shock, looked on.

Niamh finally responded to her mother's command to drop the bike.

"Run, Niamh, run," her mother urged again, "run home, run home and lock the door."

As Niamh did her mother's bidding Mrs. McGillicuddy jumped on the front wheel of the bike before lunging at Mrs. O'Riordan, gouging her face with her nails, tearing the bodice of her frock to flitters.

At last salvation came. Sergeant McGillicuddy caught hold of the flaying arms and pressed them to his wife's sides. Holding her firmly and strongly, muttering soothing words, he led her away from the mangled bicycle and his shaking, trembling neighbour.

*

But the move to the larger ground floor flat, away from the raging Mrs. McGillicuddy, brought new problems.

A man addicted to drink headed the family that moved into the flat vacated by the O'Riordan's. Private Maguire was the living embodiment of the evils of drink. He drank often and to excess. It was the general consensus that he was so far gone he'd lick alcohol off a scabby leg. In drink he was violent and abusive and cowardly. He did not pose a physical threat to anyone except his wife and young family, but neighbours were forced, time and again, to listen to the punches and kicks, the screams of terror and pain, the horrific streams of abuse.

On the few occasions, late at night, when Mrs. Maguire managed to escape the violence, she sought shelter with Mrs. O'Riordan who, unlike other neighbours, had befriended the unfortunate woman. In response to the desperate knocking on her door Mrs. O'Riordan leapt from her bed and, in fear and trembling, ushered the bruised and bleeding woman into the sanctuary of her home. But Mrs. Maguire could not stay long. She was tended to as well as was possible and bundled out the back window.

Enraged that his quarry had escaped, Private Maguire staggered along the veranda, down the stairs, along the path and set up a howl outside Mrs. O'Riordan's locked door.

The men of the barracks did not intervene in these episodes. What happened in a man's home was his affair. If Mrs. Maguire had a problem with her husband she should report him to the authorities; it wasn't their job to rat on anyone.

*

In all her long life Niamh remembered several occasions when she had been angry with her father, but she could only recall one occasion when she had burned with shame on his behalf, and it had to do with the Maguires.

It was a cold winter's evening and her father had built a roaring log fire that filled the living room with shafts of dancing light and the heady smell of burning wood. Niamh and her brothers sat on the floor, their parents in sagging armchairs either side of the hearth. Apart from the gleaming flames there was no other light in the room. As on many previous occasions, their father entranced them with the story of Oisín and the *Fianna*. They listened with rapt attention as he told them of the wanderings of the legendary heroes; of battles fought with enormous courage, strength and skill; of Oisín's sojourn in *Tír na nÓg*, The Land of Youth, where time stood still. "After a while in that enchanted fairyland Oisín longed for home, longed to see his family," their father told them. "Oisín thought he had been away for just three years, when sure hadn't he had been away for three hundred? Oisín's wife gave him Embar, her magical horse, to take him to the land of mortals. She warned that he must not set foot on the earth, for if he did he would never return to *Tír na nÓg* and would never see her again. So off he went astride the snowy-white horse, its long silky mane flowing in the wind as it galloped over the sea and back to Ireland."

Their father paused, puffed on his pipe, blew a tendril of smoke into the air. "But Oisín's good nature caused his downfall," he continued. "Mounted on his horse he tried to help some men lift a heavy rock. He slipped from his saddle and fell to the ground. In an instant he had changed from a handsome young warrior to an old man with a long beard who couldn't even see the hand in front of his face. And he never returned to *Tír na nÓg*, never saw his beautiful wife again."

Into the hush that followed the end of their father's storytelling, came screams of real terror from the flat above, and they knew that Mr. Maguire was on the rampage. They sat for a while, tense and quiet as their pleasure ebbed away.

Unable to endure the horror of her neighbour's pain Mrs. O'Riordan jumped from her chair. "Will nobody help that poor woman?" she cried, looking pointedly towards her husband.

"You don't interfere in other people's business," he said.

"If it was your daughter you'd want someone to have the gumption to interfere," her mother spat the words at him. She wrenched the front door open and ran into the road and Niamh heard her furious shout.

"Leave that woman alone, you drunken bowsie. You'll burn in hell, you cowardly blackguard."

Her father rose from his chair, put on his greatcoat and pushed past her mother as she returned to the living room, her face red with cold and anger.

The ache and throbbing in her head could no doubt be attributed to too much alcohol (her mother would be delighted to know) and the aches and pains in her bones to the four little gurriers who'd flattened her on the strand, but it was the sixth day of her trip and she hadn't covered half her route so there was no time for slacking. She had to be up and about.

With a good deal of effort she climbed out of bed and headed towards the bathroom. Following her usual practice she avoided looking in the mirror so failed to spot the bump on her forehead and the bruise that circled her right eye.

Having showered, she sat on the side of the bed and pulled on her jeans. When she'd finished dressing she put *Ulysses* into her bag — she couldn't leave without her talisman — even though it weighed a ton. Joyce was a self-centred sod, producing a bloody great tome like that without a thought for his readers and the damage it could do to a woman's wrists as she tried to hold the great thing for hours on end.

Suddenly she stopped her moaning self in her tracks; she remembered her invitation to Elizabeth in the early hours of the morning. "Damn and blast," she muttered. She couldn't hope to complete her journey with the drunken academic in tow — she'd probably want to stop at every pub *en route*. "I know, I'll skip breakfast, slip out of the hotel and pretend I forgot because I was the worse for wear."

Niamh closed her room door, quietly, turned towards the lift and almost fell over Elizabeth's outstretched body.

"What are you doing down there?"

"I haven't a notion," Elizabeth gave an embarrassed laugh, "but don't worry. I can sleep anywhere; I've had years of practice. Are you all set for breakfast? I could eat the rear end of a cow through a hedge."

"Hang on a minute," Niamh said. She slipped into her room and divested herself of her good-luck charm.

*

They tucked into a full Irish breakfast, served by the charming Spanish waitress.

"What's the story, then?" Elizabeth wanted to know as she drank her third cup of coffee.

"I planned to walk a set route on this trip, but I've fallen behind schedule so I've decided to use the DART. I covered Sandymount, Booterstown, Blackrock and Seapoint yesterday before I was deflected. Today I want to reach Killiney. I get off the train at each station, walk around a bit, get back on the train and then head for the next station."

"There must be a point to such an apparently pointless exercise." Elizabeth gave Niamh a quizzical look. "But sure I'll ask no questions then you'll tell me no lies."

*

They caught the DART at Booterstown, but not before Elizabeth had insisted they exchange mobile numbers. "In case I lose you in the crowds," she explained.

As they had made a late start because of their disturbed night, the sun had already burnt off the early mist and was shining brightly from a clear blue sky. The train rattled along and they sat in silence, enjoying the coastal view.

They passed Blackrock and Seapoint. Salthill was the next stop and their first port of call. The train slowed and Elizabeth rose to disembark.

"Ah, feck it," said Niamh, "I think I'll leave it. I've never been to Salthill in my life and there's no need to start now."

They alighted from the train at Dun Laoghaire and made their way to the pier. "I hate this godforsaken place," Elizabeth said. "It always brings to mind the hundreds and thousands of poor creatures who were forced to leave Ireland in search of a better life."

"That was a long time ago and best forgotten." Niamh walked briskly on.

"If it's best forgotten, why are you here? What's this trip if not an act of remembrance?"

*

Back on the train they sat without speaking, catching intermittent glimpses of the sea as it lapped the rocks and sandy beaches. Elizabeth's remark about the legacy of Dun Laoghaire had hit a tender spot. Like Joyce, Niamh had left Ireland with the love of her life; had departed from this port, her large family waving frantically, shouting their farewells, tears flowing in torrents. "We'll come soon, so we will," they promised fervently. They must have taken a very circuitous route, Niamh thought. Forty-five years later she was still waiting for them to show up.

As they approached Sandycove, Elizabeth broke the silence. "I'm assuming you'll want to get off here," she said, "and pay homage to the bold Joyce."

They alighted once again, walking stiffly now, their rough night catching up with them. It was a fair walk to Link Road and then they had to take a right into Marine Parade and there it was, still a good distance away, the Martello Tower, standing robust and solid in the bright sunshine. Niamh led the way, excited to be here at last.

She had seen the Tower many times on previous visits but had been singularly uninterested in the circular stone structure, one of many built by the British to protect the eastern shores of Ireland. For her it was just another symbol of the country's colonial past and something to be ignored. But in making the tower home to Buck Mulligan and Stephen in the opening pages of *Ulysses* she felt Joyce had reclaimed it for the Irish, a process that had been completed by *Bord Fáilte* when they created a museum to the writer within its sturdy walls.

Niamh no longer sought out museums and galleries as assiduously as she once had: being a culture vulture may have been good for the spirit, but it was hard on the legs. However, she felt sure she could muster the energy to cope with the tiny museum that stood directly in front of her, bounded on one side by rocks and the pounding waves.

"You go," Elizabeth said, lighting one of her foul-smelling cigars, "I've seen it many times. I'll wait here."

Niamh studied the contents of the glass cases that furnished the downstairs room — first editions of the great man's work, including the original *Ulysses*. She looked at the many photographs of Joyce and his family and friends and the pictures that had been inspired by his work: was particularly struck by the up-front (or bare-arsed) vulgarity of Bloom in Nighttown by Eamon O'Doherty, depicting the prostrate Bloom's bare bum and the overblown semi-naked women of his imaginings. She also spent some time taking in the layout of the first-floor room where Joyce slept when he had spent, a not entirely happy, six days with St. John Gogarty and his Anglo-Irish friend.

Conscious that Elizabeth was waiting she decided not to climb to the next level.

*

"Perhaps we could leave Dalkey until the return journey?" Niamh suggested. "I wouldn't insist on stopping there, but I just love the harbour and it's a place I've visited often over the years."

"No problem," Elizabeth replied.

They were on their way to Killiney and the train that had been almost empty until then was filled to bursting by a crowd of basketball players. The youngsters piled into the carriage, rushing to claim seats. "That seat is intended for the elderly," a frail old man pointed out to a youngster in sports trousers and hooded top, who vacated it with ill grace.

When they reached their destination Niamh and Elizabeth forced their way through the crush of bodies and onto the platform.

"What's the story, then?" Elizabeth asked.

"I thought we could lunch at the hotel and then enjoy a leisurely stroll along the beach."

"You'll be lucky."

"What do you mean?"

"There's no hotel?"

"If that's your idea of a joke it's not funny."

"Sure why would I joke about a thing like that? There's no hotel."

"Since when?"

"Since it was turned into luxury apartments."

"Dear god, is nothing sacred?"

"I'm assuming that you don't really want an answer to that question," Elizabeth said." I'm assuming that now is not the moment you'd choose to discuss the sanctity of an object, person or institution?"

"For Christ's sake stop your senseless academic blather. I'm starving. Where are we going to eat? Why didn't you tell me sooner, before we landed in this godforsaken hole?"

"So Killiney is no longer the most beautiful place on earth, the place where you feel more at peace than any where else in the entire world? As soon as your belly is empty the wonders of nature cease to be of consequence. The most important thing is filling your gob."

"At least I'm not shaking from head to toe because I've had to do without a drink for an hour."

Too late Niamh shut her mouth. Elizabeth lowered her head and her body trembled. The trembling grew into a violent shaking and Elizabeth buried her face in her hands.

"I'm sorry, I'm sorry." Niamh ran to her, held her, but she continued to shake. "I'm so sorry," Niamh cried. "That was unforgivable. This trip was a bad idea. It's doing me head in."

Elizabeth emitted a strangled sob and collapsed onto the platform.

"Oh, my god," Niamh shouted. "Help, somebody help me," but there was nobody there to respond to her call.

"Dear lord, dear lord," the words came from the little bundle on the platform and Niamh knelt beside her.

Elizabeth struggled into a sitting position. "Dear lord," she repeated, "that's the best laugh I've had in years." She pointed to Niamh's face. "That bump on your forehead and that black circle round your eye are ridiculous; you look as though you've done a couple of rounds with Mohammad Ali."

And she was off again. Niamh sat next to her and joined in.

"I can't believe homeless drunks have reached Killiney," an outraged passenger who had just arrived with her husband complained as she stepped round the two women. "It's time the government put a stop to immigration. The country is being infested by the scum of the earth."

Elizabeth looked at Niamh. Niamh looked at Elizabeth and they were off again, sending great peals of laughter into the salty air.

Despite the best efforts of the Gaelic Athletic Association to promote Gaelic football and hurling among Irish boys in the 1950s, the most popular sport for the boys of Cathal Brugha Barracks came from across the Atlantic.

Basketball had been introduced to the Irish army by Sergeant Major Doogan in 1923, but really took off after an American base was established in Derry in the north of Ireland during the Second World War (or the Emergency as it was known in Eire).

Irish service men, infatuated by the glamour of the American game, amazed themselves by showing an aptitude for it. Matches were arranged between the teams at various barracks throughout the country and, no doubt with some trepidation, the gauntlet was thrown down to the Yanks themselves. The twice-yearly Blitz was established — fierce knockout competitions that began early in the morning and finished when the best, or most brutal team, triumphed.

The Number One Army Band emerged as the premier military team in Cathal Brugha Barracks and their matches with the Yanks drew capacity crowds in what was, it has to be admitted, a not particularly large gymnasium.

The young women of the barracks, dressed to the nines in swirling skirts, hair styled in elaborate *bouffants*, tripped daintily past the Cross Gate, took a left at the Band Room and arrived at the Gym, giggling and expectant. Their knowledge of the game was not great, but it was not the game that interested them. The main event for them was the sight of the tall tanned gum-chewing Yanks, kitted out in satin shorts and co-ordinating vests that clung to well-toned physiques.

As far as Niamh knew none of the Yanks had bagged a young woman from married quarters. The conditions were against them: the visits lasted one day and most of that time the men were busy running up and down a court, trying desperately to sink a ball into a basket. Besides, most of the men were already fixed up with a Derry lass and also, no doubt, with the girl next door back in the States.

The frisson of excitement that accompanied the Americans was enjoyed by almost everyone, not just the young women. The mothers who ventured forth knew a fine piece of beefcake when they saw it. They didn't often get the chance to feast their eyes so they looked forward to the twice-yearly visits. The kids loved the Yanks. "Hey, mister gis some chewing gum," they shouted, and were amazed when their demands were met, not with a clip round the ear, but with handfuls of the stuff thrown into the air.

For the players of the Number One Army Band Basketball Team there was more at stake than winning a sporting tournament. They looked forward to the visits with mixed feelings: they were terrified that they might disgrace themselves, that the towering Americans might wipe the floor with them; they dreamed of the possibility of turning the tables and demolishing the brash, swaggering opposition, of humiliating them. The rewards for such a triumph would be great: the local women would see to that.

*

The realization that if they wanted a piece of the action they would have to learn the foreign game came late to the lads from married-quarters and their team, The Dodgers, was formed, followed over the years by The Tigers and Celtic. They were given permission to train in the army gym where, surprisingly quickly, they honed their skills and a great rivalry was born — from here on in the lads from the band and the lads from the other side of the railings were bitter opponents on the basketball court and in the field of love.

As the game grew in popularity married quarters resounded to the sound of bouncing basketballs. On summer evenings teenage lads showed off their skills to watching mothers who sat on doorsteps, enjoying the evening sun. But the dodging and swerving, the feints and dummies were not performed just to impress their mothers; their target was the group of girls who watched from a distance; their purpose was to close the gap between themselves and the young woman, to get in close, to feel the warmth of their soft young bodies.

Observing her brothers and their friends, Niamh noticed that the sequence of events that led to the closing of the gap followed the same pattern each evening. The boys displayed their skills, ignoring the watching girls. The girls laughed and pointed, draping themselves against a wall, fence, pole or any convenient structure. When the noise coming from the female quarter reached a certain pitch a boy threw the ball carelessly. The ball landed close to the girls' circle and they pounced on it with whoops and peals of laughter. The ball was thrown back. This sequence was repeated until the space between the ball-throwing lads and the giggling girls decreased and somehow they were all joined in a noisy *mêlée* where hands touched, body brushed against body, the swirling, perfumed hair of a girl stroked the pimply cheek of a teenage boy.

The watching Niamh could see no sense in the game.

"They're stupid," she said to her mother. "They should have proper teams. How can they keep the score?" And she was infuriated by her mother's reply.

"Don't worry, *a stór*," she laughed, "they'll find a way."

*

The rivalry between the Army School of Music's basketball team and the team from the married-quarters was the cause of many a family rift; young women were forced to choose between supporting a boyfriend or a brother. Niamh's brothers proved to have a talent for the game and from the age of sixteen to nineteen she courted a band-boy, so she was faced with an uncomfortable choice.

"Now what?" her mother challenged.

"No contest," Niamh answered, "I've always supported my brothers; I'm not going to change now."

"You won't be marrying him then," was her mother's exasperating response.

*

Her eldest brother's greatest sporting triumph had taken place a couple of years before she was forced to decide where her loyalties lay, and she had missed the moment.

In 1957 Ireland was chosen to host The European Catholic Student Games. Basketball was one of the designated sports and Ireland was expected to play. The sport was not on the curriculum of the National Schools so the team was chosen from the leading private schools. There was only one problem; their players were rubbish.

A dilemma for the selection committee.

But hold your horses, weren't there some lads in the barracks who were handy when it came to throwing a ball into a basket?

But didn't those lads work? I mean they weren't students.

Think again.

Enquire further.

God bless us.

Sure aren't they students after all.

Two of them do day-release at Bolton Street Tech and one of them attends night classes at Rathmines High School.

Thanks be to god.

That settled, Daniel captained the Irish team and the O'Riordan family swelled with pride; Mrs. O'Riordan's feet didn't touch the ground for a fortnight and Mr. O'Riordan allowed himself the odd smile.

But there was humiliation in store. The teams from continental Europe came kitted out to beat the band. They were only gorgeous. Matching kit, tracksuits, bags; their country's name emblazoned in gold on everything, while the Irish had hardly a vest and knickers between them.

The scalding shame of it!

Cleary's to the rescue: they lent each player of the entire Irish squad — track, field and basketball teams — a couple of pairs of shorts, vests and a tracksuit.

And then there was the matter of winning a game or two.

Luxemburg and, the second favourites, Spain, beat the Irish basketball team, led by her brother, in front of the home crowd, in their first two games. Niamh watched in an agony of mixed emotions: fear, pride, expectation, exhilaration, as Daniel and his team fought like tigers to prevail over their opponents.

But no luck.

They were beaten — only just — they'd done themselves and their nation proud, had given their all, so no shame in that.

Although it would be some time before Rotter's theory on locus of control was published, Niamh had an instinctive grasp of the phenomenon. She convinced herself that she was responsible for both defeats, that her attendance at the games resulted in the defeat of Daniel and his players, that she had the power to jinx the team. Consequently, she made a decision that she would regret all her life. She decided, for the good of her brother and of Ireland, that she would miss the next game.

*

Portugal was the favourite to win the tournament. The team not only looked scrumptious, they played with dazzling speed and ball-handling wizardry.

They had watched, with patronizing boredom, on the two occasions when Ireland went down to defeat. On the night of their match with the home nation they ran onto the court exuding manly arrogance, overbearing confidence. Relaxed and assured they warmed up, throwing the ball languidly, aware of the stir they caused, particularly among the young women.

The Irish team, led by Daniel, joined them. It was do or die; they had nothing to lose; no point in hanging back; forget about tactics, about containing their opponents, just go for it.

And they did. And the crowd swelled with pride as the Irish lads sank ball after ball. The roof almost flew to the heavens with the roars they let out. But Niamh was not there to witness the glory of it. A couple of hundred yards away she sat with Philomena in D Block, knowing something wondrous was taking place, wanting with every fibre of her being to run and witness it, but forcing herself to stay where she was because she didn't want to put the mockers on it, didn't want to jeopardize her brother's victory.

When she was sure the final whistle had been blown she took flight; ran and ran and ran towards the Gym where the crowd were dancing and cheering, fit to die from the joy of it. The people of the barracks were the most vocal in their delight. Their team had beaten the favourites and sure weren't the three best players from the married-quarters, and wasn't the captain one of them?

Sláinte!

And the Portuguese conquistadores were in the changing, room drained of arrogance, crying like babies.
Sláinte!
Arís, agus arís, agus arís!

They sat on a mound of pebbles a couple of yards from the water's edge, eating sandwiches and drinking tea that they had bought from the shop on the beach. As Niamh looked out to sea, mesmerized by the powerful curling waves which roared onto the shingle, sending fountains of spray into the air, she imagined an enchanted white horse, tail and mane flying in the wind, galloping over the waves, carrying its rider home. She heard the soft lilt of her father's voice as he sat in the circle of his family, flames leaping from the fire he had built, sharing with them the stories of ancient Ireland.

"Tell me now, why do you love this place so much?"

"Need you ask?" Niamh swivelled her head one hundred and eighty degrees to the left and then to the right, taking in the sweep of the bay. "It's magnificent," she said, "simply magnificent."

"Granted it has a certain appeal, but you must have come across better in your travels."

"In terms of scale, yes; in terms of natural beauty, no."

"You can't tell me that San Francisco Bay or the Bay at Nice, or any of a dozen places in Greece is not better endowed by nature than Killiney."

Niamh chewed on a piece of bread, keeping her gaze on the foaming surf. "You're right of course," she said. "It's not simply the beauty of a place that makes us love it, makes us pine for it when we're elsewhere. It's all the associations, all the memories we make in a certain place that imprints it on our hearts and on our minds."

They continued to eat in silence until the food had gone. There were very few others on the strand — a lone walker here and there; two brave souls battling against the surf and, downwind of them, a group of seniors sitting, chatting and laughing.

"I first came to Killiney as a teenager," Niamh said. "One Sunday, against orders, Deirdre and I cycled all the way from Rathmines. I think we were trying to find Bray, but we were hopeless at navigation, didn't know there was such a thing, so we ended up on the Vico Road. Of course we couldn't stay mounted, so we pushed our bikes up the hill until we found our way to the beach. We loved it. In those days it was deserted so we thought it was our secret place and we came as often as we could."

*

They strolled along the beach towards Dalkey and were soon cut off by the tide; a change of direction brought Bray Head into view.

"Do you have a favourite place," Niamh asked, "or is that a foolish question?"

"Sure when you have attachments to as many places as I have, it's difficult to decide." Elizabeth stopped and considered for a moment. "I suppose I love the place I'm in at a given time."

"That's a good trick if you can pull it off."

"By god you're right, but like all survival strategies it was hard won."

By mutual consent and without saying a word, they sat once again on the shingle. They breathed deeply, soaking up the tranquil atmosphere, enjoying the warmth of the October sun, tuning into the sound of pounding surf; lulled by it all to the brink of sleep.

*

They were on the DART, with just one more stop before they could chug towards Booterstown and their hotel. They had dozed awhile on the strand, walked stiffly to the station and waited ten minutes for the train to arrive. They disembarked at Dalkey and strolled through the narrow streets, past Elsinore (a house which jutted out over the sea) to the tiny Coliemore Harbour where a few boats lay on the slip and a young woman cast a line from the stone jetty. As Niamh watched the fisher-woman, she imagined her father's shape, shimmering and indistinct, rising from the water, carrying aloft his most prized catch — a gleaming sea bass.

Elizabeth sank onto a wooden bench on the cobbled area next to the sea wall while Niamh stood, gazing at yet another Martello Tower that soared above the ruins of St. Begnal's Church on nearby Dalkey Island. The thought struck her that these structures provided an apt metaphor for the relationship between colonizer and colonized: windowless, sturdy, circular, they loomed over the conquered land, confident, unseeing, uncaring; promising domination without end.

She made to join Elizabeth on the pretty terrace with its tastefully designed seats and tubs of pink and white verbena, but as she was about to take the weight off her feet the heavens opened and they were forced to hurry to the station.

*

Back on the train again and they sat in silence, Niamh devouring the passing scene, attempting to satisfy a longing that she knew could never be assuaged; Elizabeth imbibing from the bottle in her bag when she thought Niamh wasn't looking.

They decided they would meet for dinner at eight — late for them — but they both agreed that their travels had tired them out so they needed a nap. "It's hard to credit that I once spent five weeks walking and living rough in Patagonia, not to mention bestowing my charms on each of the guides in turn. A civilized people, the Patagonians, and the men are so tall," Elizabeth said, with a lusty chuckle as she parted from Niamh at the lift.

*

Her itinerary was in flitters. She hadn't glanced at *Ulysses* for almost two days; apart from a few notes she hadn't written anything and her walking schedule was way off course. She must have been mad to suggest Elizabeth tag along. It had put the mockers on everything. At best she had about three hours reading time and five hours walking time left. She'd have to try and shake her off somehow, although that would be difficult, she was like a barnacle: once she got hold she clung on for dear life. Well she could sod off. She would let her know over dinner, in no uncertain terms, that she needed to complete her trip around Dublin on her own.

She lay on the bed, picked up the book and started to read, determined to make up for lost time.

*

They tucked into their food with gusto: Niamh ate lemon sole, chips and a fresh green salad and drank water; Elizabeth ate her usual disgusting coddle and slurped a large whiskey.

The dining room was busy; the young, mostly foreign staff, ran to and fro, attempting to satisfy the demands of all the diners simultaneously.

"The slaves of advanced capitalism," Elizabeth muttered.

"You what?" Niamh looked at her in surprise.

"Aren't the people who work in the service industry the slaves of advanced capitalism?"

"I know they're not well paid, but that's a long way from slavery."

"Have you ever worked in a kitchen or as a waitress?"

"Well, my own kitchen, of course, but no, I've never been a waitress."

"Well don't talk bullshite, then. I'm telling you these young people are treated abominably and what's more …" As she spoke Elizabeth waved her hand in a grand flourish, lost her balance and fell from her chair.

With a cry of alarm Niamh was on her feet and moved as quickly as her stiff limbs allowed to the other side of the table.

"Excuse me, excuse me," Niamh called to a passing waiter, but he either didn't hear or was beyond caring. She caught Elizabeth firmly by the arm and pulled with all her might.

"Stand up, "she said, "Stand up, and I'll get you a black coffee."

*

"I'm not that drunk," Elizabeth said, when she was seated once again. She looked at Niamh, her brown eyes serious. "I meant it when I said that these youngsters are exploited. But sure then the Irish are good at slavery."

Niamh opened her mouth to protest, but Elizabeth would not shut up. Slavers, she insisted, came in many guises and just because Ireland had never shipped slaves overseas like Britain and other European powers did not mean they had not enslaved people in modern times. Wasn't it well known that thousands of young women were kept against their will in the most abominable conditions, working as hard as any slave in laundries run by the nuns, the skin of their knuckles scraped to the bone from the boiling water and the scrubbing of clothes, not allowed to see anyone from the outside world, not even allowed to comfort each other and wasn't all this tolerated by the government, the church and the families of the poor unfortunate women? And it only coming to light when the nuns sold off some land and the bodies of over a hundred women were found. And what was their crime? Why was this acceptable to the population at large? Because the poor young ones were sexually active. As if being sexually active was unnatural. If that wasn't slavery then what was?

Niamh lowered her head as Elizabeth's voice rose higher and higher, reaching a pitch about two octaves above middle C (she was taking piano lessons so she knew something of music). There was an uneasy shifting amongst other diners.

"I don't know about you," Niamh said, "but I'm exhausted, I'm off to bed. Tomorrow's my last day and I have a lot to pack in."

"All this rushing about will do you no good," Elizabeth said in a heavily slurred voice. "If you stay for a few more days you'll have plenty of time for your maudlin meanderings." She paused then finished with a flourish, "How about that then?" she said.

Niamh didn't answer. She took Elizabeth by the elbow and, applying pressure in an upward direction, levered her from the chair, then half carried, half dragged her as far as the lift, propped her against the wall until the lift arrived, out at the sixth floor, more dragging and carrying, fumbled in Elizabeth's pocket for her key, opened the door and flung her onto the bed.

Up early the next morning Niamh hurried downstairs to check her emails. W.B. was still urging her to make the trip to his city. His grandma's health had deteriorated and he wasn't sure how long she would last and she was, apparently, very keen to make Niamh's acquaintance. All her friends from home had passed away and she would give her eye-teeth (though Niamh would be surprised if she still had them) to talk to someone who had grown up in Dublin at the same time as she.

She sat eating breakfast, pleased Elizabeth was nowhere in sight. "I wouldn't go to New York if you beamed me up and landed me in that fair metropolis in a matter of seconds," Niamh addressed the absent W.B.

*

As a child she had listened, trembling with fright and excitement, as her mother told of how her parents and older brothers and sisters had been forced from their cottage in the west of Ireland and onto the roadside while the Black and Tans searched and then wrecked the house because they had failed to find members of the IRA for whom they were looking. Her father and brothers had been roughed up, punched and kicked: her sisters humiliated (her mother did not expand on this aspect of the proceedings). But they were lucky to get away with their lives: the day before a man had been killed in nearby Milltown Malbay and eight houses were burnt down. The Tans, continuing their rampage shot a man and boy in Ennistymon and razed more buildings to the ground.

So Niamh's aunts and uncles, with the blessing of their heart-broken parents, set off on their arduous journey from Queenstown. They settled in New York, worked long and hard; endured the bitter loneliness and grinding poverty of the emigrant; coped with terrible tragedy (one aunt's son, whilst in the care of a child-minder, had fallen into a furnace and burned to death). They had survived and prospered materially, but their dream of earning enough money to return and settle in Ireland had never been realized and they had died far from home filled, until the end, with a deep longing for the soft green hills and the wild pounding ocean of their native county.

"Sentimental blather," Niamh's mother declared when she read of this longing in the rare letters that arrived from across the Atlantic. "I'd like to see how long they'd last in the soft green hills without their cars, washing machines and refrigerators. I'd give them a month at most before they rushed pell-mell back to the States." But her cynicism could not hide the mixture of envy and melancholy in her voice.

Although she had never met them, never even seen photographs of these relations, Niamh had missed them. They had been an absence in her life where there should have been a presence. She had aunts, uncles, cousins somewhere in the world that she would never meet, never know, and the thought filled her with sadness.

In her third year at the University of Birmingham the drama students had mounted a production of Israel Zangwill's *The Melting Pot*. The acting was pretty crap and the accents dire, but it had been seared on her memory because of just one line of dialogue. "America," one of the characters had declaimed, "is the great melting-pot where all the races of Europe are melting and reforming." She supposed it had affected her so deeply because many of her family had melted into that pot. For some time after seeing the play her sleep had been disturbed by nightmares of her aunts and uncles imprisoned in a great cauldron, writhing in agony as their flesh dissolved and then fused into unrecognizable lumps.

*

She hurried from the dining room, into the lift and along the corridor to her room. Good: still no sign of Elizabeth. If she put a spurt on she could make her escape. She had so little time left she couldn't afford to be hampered in her progress; she needed to be out there, fulfilling her mission.

She brushed her teeth, stepped out of the bathroom and stopped dead. The room was as dark as a tomb; she could hardly see her hand in front of her face.

She inched her way towards the window and sighed with relief when she saw the cause of the funereal gloom. For a minute there she'd thought that she'd lost her sight, but it was just a spate of local weather that was causing the problem.

A doom-laden sky vented its fury on Dublin; it unleashed torrents of rain that drummed against the window, swirled along the paths below and overflowed the drains. The sea refused to take this outburst lying down: a heaving mass of grey, edged with foaming white, it soared and swelled in retaliation. Like a spoilt child, the wind joined in: determined to be noticed, it howled and shrieked, buffeting the waves into great cascades of water and tearing branches from trees.

Niamh's relief was short-lived. There was no way she could complete her walk around Rathmines in this weather; she'd be soaked to the skin, blown off her pins, not to mention being sent reeling into the channel. And then she remembered Elizabeth's suggestion, "If you stay a few more days you'll have plenty of time for your maudlin meanderings," she'd said, rather rudely. But then what could you expect from a drunk?

*

Elizabeth found her curled up on a comfy sofa in the foyer, reading *Ulysses*.

"You can always rely on Ireland to piss on the righteous," she said. "I'm sorry you won't be able to complete your ramblings."

"You mean my maudlin meanderings."

"Well, I wouldn't be the one to call them that, but ...."

"Oh, don't worry; I'll have plenty of time to finish what I came to do. I took your advice; I'm staying another few days."

The folds of Elizabeth's face puckered into a beaming smile and her brown eyes danced. "That calls for a celebration: I think I'll have a large one."

*

They read for a while in companionable silence. Every now and then Elizabeth gave a satisfied chuckle, took a sip from her glass, wriggled a bit in her chair then settled down to read some more.

"That must be an amusing book," Niamh remarked, looking over the rim of her glasses.

"Ah, sure it's all right."

"Why all the sniggering then?"

"Can't a woman feel pleased with herself and express that pleasure without being taken to task?"

"Feel as pleased as you like."

"How are you getting on with the bold Joyce?" Elizabeth asked ten minutes later.

"Fine."

Elizabeth let out a roar of laughter. "You're not sulking are you? Please tell me a woman of your age has grown out of sulking?"

For a brief moment Niamh considered taking umbrage at being ridiculed, but found she couldn't be bothered.

"I'm reading Molly's soliloquy. It's utterly compelling."

"Hot stuff, eh?"

"Not just that. Not just the bold sweep of it, the fearless honesty of the writing, the … the…" Niamh stumbled to a halt and then started up again. "I mean, what is truly extraordinary is that a man could know women so well, could capture every facet of the female personality so accurately. I've never read anything like it in my entire life. It is …" she stumbled again, searching for the word, the phrase that would express what she wanted to say. "It's a revelation, truly amazing."

"How about that then?" Elizabeth laughed. "Even after all this time Joyce can still get the old juices flowing."

*

They took turns walking to the door to check on the weather. The rain continued to fall in sheets and the wind continued to howl, so they gave up all hope of an outing; they would just have to dig in, stay put. Although the bus that would take them into town stopped directly outside the hotel they feared while awaiting its arrival they might be knocked sideways by the strong winds, or worse still, be blown skywards, clinging to their umbrellas, two aged Mary Poppins, swept out over the bay. That's if the bus ever arrived. The Dublin bus service was not renowned for its reliability.

At twelve-thirty they adjourned to the bar for lunch. Niamh ordered a cheese and tomato toastie; Elizabeth a small portion of stinking coddle.

"Let's go to a singles' club tonight," Elizabeth suggested between spoonfuls of the highly flavoured stew.

"You what?" Niamh's eyes popped in amazement.

"An over seventies singles' club."

"Have you taken leave of your senses?"

"No offence, but my guess is that you are single and there's no need to worry about the age thing, sure nobody will take a blind bit of notice if you don't meet the requirement, don't they love a bit of younger flesh."

"They don't have singles clubs for the over seventies," Niamh countered.

Wrong move.

Elizabeth assured her that such organizations did indeed exist all over Ireland and by the dozen in Dublin. It was one of the better ideas that had come out of America, had been fuelled by a miracle of medical science — the one, the only, the amazing, Viagra. A far-seeing geriatric in Miami (figuratively speaking that is — far-seeing in the sense that he saw the drug's potential for himself and the other inmates at the home, but not far-seeing in so far as looking to the future because of course he didn't really have much of a future). Anyway, the magical pill had worked wonders and now Vs were the mature clubbers Es and the incident of venereal disease in seventy to ninety year olds far exceeded that of fourteen to twenty-five year olds. "How about that then?" she beamed.

"Have you taken leave of your senses?" Niamh asked again, stuck in a groove of disbelief. "Are you trying to tell me that the fact that hundreds …"

"Thousands," Elizabeth interjected.

"… thousands of old people have contracted deadly diseases like gonorrhoea and syphilis, diseases that could result in blindness or …or …even madness is a good thing?"

"Of course it's a good thing. I'm not advocating it for those with their lives ahead of them — not at all, but why not for the old. Most of them are half blind or half mad anyway and I don't suppose any of the women will become pregnant so they might as well enjoy their last years."

"But, but they could …" Niamh searched for a counter argument. "They could die of a heart attack."

"Which would you choose," Elizabeth raised an ironic eyebrow, "dying on the job in paroxysms of delight or lingering in a hospital ward if you're lucky, or on a trolley in a corridor if you're not? Have you any idea how terrible the medical care is in this country? And anyway it's a well-known syndrome."

"What is?" As soon as she'd asked the question Niamh regretted it. She didn't want to know the answer. Elizabeth's blather was getting out of hand. The drink was driving her insane.

"Oldies dying on the job; it's called sex suicide."

While Niamh attempted to catch her breath Elizabeth delivered another broadside.

"Hubert is taking it," she said.

"Don't be ridiculous, that man can hardly walk."

"Not surprising, after the night we spent together," Elizabeth gave a joyful laugh.

"Now I know you're having me on. You were so drunk I had to carry you to your room and put you on your bed?"

"Throw me, you mean. I don't call standing in the doorway and giving a person a violent shove, putting them to bed. Anyway, it was your rough handling that made me wake up so I had plenty of time to prepare for my ten o'clock assignation with Hubert."

*

As soon as possible after lunch and with the rain continuing to lash the city in punitive torrents Niamh made her escape to her room.

Glad to return to the comparative sanity of Joyce's Dublin, she lay on her bed and resumed her reading of *Ulysses*.

Try as she would Niamh could not rid herself of the lurid images evoked by Elizabeth's ravings. (Surely she had to be raving?) The information her tiny acquaintance had imparted had induced a state of the utmost mental turmoil.

The mere idea of geriatrics going at it like dogs on heat made her cringe in disgust. Simultaneously, at the very moment she was shuddering with distaste, she berated herself for her prudery, her hypocrisy. Her liberal beliefs easily embraced the notion of sexually active seniors. Every adult, she would argue, should be able to express their sexuality as they saw fit, provided they did it in private with another, or even other consenting adults. But the idea evoked by Elizabeth of a permanently erect member ready to skewer an ever-ready vagina filled her with distaste, but only if the member and vagina belonged to the old. If the bodies going at it hammer and tongs were young, firm and luscious she found the idea pleasing and somewhat arousing.

Anger at Elizabeth bubbled, foamed and frothed. Why couldn't the little weirdo keep her perverted proclivities to herself; why did she have to taint everyone else with her debauchery?

Niamh's reaction was over the top and she knew it. She knew also that it mirrored her response when she was first introduced to the concept of sex: of how babies were conceived.

*

"Excuse me, Sister, *tá ceist agam*," Bridget Moran raised her hand and smiled sweetly at the young nun who stood at the front of the class. Bridget had warned her friends of her intention, but they hadn't believed she would go through with it, have the bare-face cheek to ask the question. "It's now or never," Bridget had said, "this one's a rookie, fresh from the African missions, she's our best bet."

"What is your question, Bridget?" the young nun asked, with an encouraging smile. A frisson of excitement rippled through the class of eleven-year-old girls. Máire Donovan looked at Blath Kerrigan who looked at Áine Shannon who giggled and looked over her shoulder at her best friend, the brave Bridget.

"What does ... what does ... the fruit of thy womb mean, sister?"

A hush descended on the class, the fidgeting of thirty young girls stopped; giggles were suppressed; coughing held in check. They hardly dared breathe as they waited for the answer.

Sister Cathal looked slightly alarmed. Her lightly tanned fair skin took on a pinkish hue, her hands fiddled with the huge rosary that hung from her waist. She coughed once, twice, and her words came in a rush. "The fruit of thy womb means the product of thy womb."

"Yes, but what does womb mean, sister," Bridget persisted.

Sister Cathal seemed not to hear. Moving swiftly to the blackboard she took a piece of chalk from the narrow shelf and started to write on the board. "Open your arithmetic books at page forty-five," she said; we'll do sums numbers one to ten."

And so ended the formal sex-education of Class Five.

*

Niamh's mother certainly never broached the subject of sex with her daughter; wouldn't dream of it. The innocence of children should be left intact was her thinking; they should be protected from the cruel realities of life for as long as possible. She seemed to forget that she herself had been born and raised on a farm where curiosity about procreation was satisfied at an early age, assuaging the fearful fascination that each generation harboured for this facet of reality. She also seemed to forget that it is not given to parents to wholly protect their children.

After the fruit of thy womb incident with Sister Cathal, the completion of Niamh's sex education came in three distinct phases.

*

It was a hot summer and the O'Riordan children were encouraged to dig a trench out the back of the flats where their mammy could keep an eye on them throughout the long school holidays. Mrs. O'Riordan calculated that if they spent three weeks digging, one week lining the trench with grass and erecting a tent over the hole with an army blanket, three weeks sitting in it, and one week putting the hardened earth back into the trench that the eight weeks of school holidays should pass without incident. But it was within the secret den — the private domain of Niamh, her brothers and their friends where admission was by password only — that Niamh learned about the realities of sex.

Her brother Paul and his friend Rabba', had been whispering and sniggering all morning and she was heartily sick of them, thinking she was the butt of their joke.

"I'm telling mammy, if you don't stop," she whined.

"Go outside," Paul ordered, "this is boys' talk."

"I will not," she said, "I helped make the den, I'm staying."

At that moment their mother's voice penetrated the walls. She needed Paul to go for messages and he was forced to leave.

"You'd better be gone by the time I get back," he warned, "or I'll drag you out."

The den was hot and airless and for the first time Niamh noticed how little space there was. She and Rabba' sat opposite each other, their bony knees almost touching. She chewed on a blade of dead grass, plucked from the floor. Rabba' tried to make his blade of grass sing, but it was too dry and his protruding front teeth (the Virgin Mary had ignored his prayers) did not lend themselves to the musical, so he made a ppiitthh sound instead. Desperately he blurted out, "I'll tell you what we were talking about if you like…me and Paul…I'll tell you, if you like."

"Okay then."

"But I'll have to whisper it," he said.

"Why?"

"Just because."

"Okay then."

Rabba' crawled towards her. He sat next to her; put his mouth close to her ear until she felt the hard enamel of his teeth against her soft flesh. His lips moved silently.

Niamh listened for a few moments and then, despite the sultry heat of the den, her small frame seemed to freeze. She felt cold sweat trickle down her back, her eyes opened wide and her mouth followed suit. Suddenly she sprang to life. She pushed Rabba' with a strength she hadn't known she possessed and scrambled out of the trench. She passed the returning Paul at break-neck speed.

"I was only joking," Paul called, "I wasn't going to hurt you."

"I'm telling mammy on you," she yelled. "I'm telling mammy what you and Rabba' O'Hare were talking about." Before she continued on her way she had the satisfaction of seeing the supercilious smirk disappear from her brother's face and a slight tinge of green creep underneath his tan.

But she had no intention of telling her mammy. She'd rather have had her tongue ripped out then repeat a word of Rabba's urgent whisperings. For months after, when his words sprang unbidden to her mind, she trembled with disgust and anger. The worst part of it was that he said her mammy and daddy did that — that all mammies and daddies did it; it was the only way to get a baby.

He was a little liar.

She wouldn't believe a word he'd said.

But Rabba' O'Hare had changed her world forever. From that day on she viewed her parents in a different light, observed closely their every move, began a futile search for evidence that would give the lie to what she'd been told.

*

Hard on the heels of Rabba's revelation came the next stage in Niamh's sex education.

Thanks to her parents' determination to protect her from the nature of human existence and to the shortcomings of the catholic educational system, she had spent her first eleven years blissfully untroubled by even the most rudimentary sexual or biological knowledge. And then, in quick succession, snippets of information were flung at her and she came to know more than she could cope with.

Two weeks into the autumn term she was walking along Leinster Road towards home in the company of Breda Mulholland and Sinead Ryan. The two girls (slightly older than Niamh) moved ahead, talking in hushed tones. Occasionally, Breda cast a glance over her shoulder at the straggling Niamh.

"What are you two whispering about?" Niamh asked, affronted at being left out of the conversation.

Breda looked at Sinead, questioningly, but Sinead shook her head.

"Can't tell you," she said, "you're too young."

"I'm nearly as old as youse," Niamh replied huffily, and before she could stop her mouth she added. "If it's about sex I know all about it; Rabba O'Hare told me."

The violence of their reaction unnerved her. Breda's mouth dropped and she looked aghast at Sinead. Sinead's eyebrows jumped as she looked askance at Niamh.

"You spoke to a boy about the curse?" Sinead was incredulous.

"He didn't say anything about a curse; he just said that mammies and daddies do it to make babies," Niamh's cheeks burned, tears started in her eyes and she could almost feel Rabba's hot breath as he whispered his obscenities into her ear.

In the end Breda and Sinead, whispering into each ear in turn, outlined a rather confusing explanation of what the curse involved.

Niamh started another tense vigil. This time her mother alone was the object of her surveillance. She scrutinized her carefully, hoping and fearing to see evidence of what her friend's had described. Paul caught her searching through the dirty washing, looking for telltale signs on her mother's knickers.

"Little gink," he hissed into her face. "I'm telling on you."

"I'm looking for my school blouse," she protested, but he wasn't convinced. For several weeks he and Daniel made a great show of jumping aside when she approached, as though fearful they might be contaminated by her touch.

Three months careful observation of her mother ended in failure. She had decided that Breda and Sinead were having her on when at last the evidence she had sought so assiduously, presented itself to her.

*

It happened at night. She was snuggled deep in her cosy bed, dreaming blissfully of swimming in a warm blue sea, of being carried towards the shore on gently lapping waves. Time and again she almost woke, almost dragged herself awake, but she was reluctant to give up the pleasure of her dreams so she snuggled deeper until, finally, the damp forced her awake. Sleepily she made her way through the dark rooms, across the icy lino, to the lavatory.

She squatted over the bowl, shivering with cold. The flow seemed unnaturally thick so she glanced down and saw a stream of bright red liquid fall onto the white porcelain. She saw streaks of red on her nightdress and ran wildly through the dark to find her mother.

Her mother, stupid with sleep, confirmed what she didn't want to believe. "It happens to every girl. You'll bleed every month from now on. You'll soon get used to it. Be a good girl and go back to bed and I'll bring you a clean nightdress and a pad."

Her mother pulled the soiled garment over Niamh's head and helped her into a fresh one. She handed her a pair of knickers, gave her a clumsy wad and told her to place it in her knickers to soak up the blood. She helped her daughter back into bed and lay next to her, gently stroking her hair until she was sure she slept.

But Niamh only pretended sleep. Long after her mother had left she lay still and cold. Her mother's touch when she had stroked her conveyed more than her usual gentle concern: it had seemed sad somehow, made Niamh feel sad too. She felt sure that she had lost something precious and that it had gone forever.

*

It was sometime after that momentous night that Niamh's sex education reached its third phase. During the intervening years more whispering and much fumbling transpired.

"Can't drag yourself away from the bold Molly's soliloquy." Elizabeth's chortle had, Niamh thought, a touch of the lewd about it and she winced in distaste.

"Actually, I've started to read the book all over again."

"She's a glutton for it." Elizabeth laughed over her shoulder, addressing Hubert whose spare frame stooped from the waist.

"What's that?" he said rather loudly, cupping his ear with his hand.

*

From lunchtime the previous day Niamh had managed to avoid contact with the irrepressible academic by remaining in her room, sleeping, eating and reading *Ulysses* — with greater understanding of at least some sections: this time round she'd found the episode in the newspaper office very amusing. But when she had stood at her window that morning, the entire bay enveloped in a thick blanket of grey cloud, rain lashing in torrents, knowing that her wanderings would have to be postponed for a further day, she felt a desperate desire to escape the dismal scene.

After breakfast she had made for the sofa in the furthest corner of the foyer, pulled on a cap to hide her fading ginger curls, covered her generously padded frame with a blanket, lay down and started to read. She read with mounting excitement and not a little trepidation. The most significant theme of the book (at least for her) was beginning to reveal itself, to make itself manifest.

"Hubert has a great idea," Elizabeth continued, "so we thought we'd run it past you."

Niamh stiffened.

She sat bolt upright.

No way was she getting involved with a three-in-a-bed stint.

Absolutely no way.

"You're obviously feeling the cold something terrible," Elizabeth said as Niamh struggled to divest herself of her cap and blanket, "so I think you'll be up for this, it'll heat you up great, won't it Hubert?"

"What's that?" Hubert cupped his ear with his hand.

Elizabeth outlined Hubert's brilliant idea. No, it wasn't a three-in-a-bed orgy, nor was it a visit to an over-seventies singles club. His idea was something else entirely. He thought it would be great fun if they visited one of the many Salsa clubs in the city. He knew of one in a basement just off Leeson Street. Not too far away and they could share a taxi. They'd have a great night, and Niamh could borrow something to wear if she didn't have anything suitable. "How about that then?" Elizabeth finally stopped for breath.

She brushed aside Niamh's protests, waving her hand as though swatting a fly. "For god's sake, don't you know your negativity is very depressing, she said, "not just for everyone around you, but for yourself as well? You'd rather sit here huddled in a corner than get out there and embrace life, have some fun and make the most of what little time you have left on this planet. You're not living in *Tír na nÓg* you know. You will actually get older and older and die. From the moment we're born we're in the game of deceiving time and the more time that passes the more urgent is the imperative. But sure if you can't see that for yourself I might as well save my breath. Come on Hubert, there are some people who just want to wallow." And off she went; her bewildered companion following in her wake.

Niamh remained in the foyer, reeling from Elizabeth's fierce salvo. Half an hour passed and she sat on. As the hands of the clock, which hung on the wall above the reception desk, moved towards the hour she rose from her seat and made for the lift.

Elizabeth opened her room door with a warm, slightly shamefaced smile. She ushered Niamh inside and an hour later ushered her out again, carrying a bright red dress, which Elizabeth assured her (not very flatteringly) would fit *Fionn mac Cumhaill*, never mind someone who was just a bit podgy. "I bought it for my neighbour in Tralee, but sure she'll never know it's been worn." To complete the outfit she had thrust a pair of what she called "shag-me shoes" at the reluctant Niamh.

*

The taxi pulled up outside a Georgian house off Leeson Street and Hubert paid the driver as Elizabeth and Niamh scurried through the rain. They stepped gingerly down the iron steps that led to the basement and pushed open the heavy door.

A blast of moist air met them as they entered the low-ceilinged room. The rhythm of Salsa vibrated around the crowded space and a scattering of couples moved to the throbbing music, the women dressed in dazzling colours, the men in dark figure-hugging shirts and pants.

The three newcomers hesitated just inside the door, trying to get their bearings. Suddenly Elizabeth was off. Like a snake, she slithered between couples, sloped beneath a raised elbow, slinked around closely packed tables.

Niamh failed to keep track of the tiny figure as she disappeared into the throng. With the advantage of height Hubert had better luck and he spotted her when she finally came to rest, close to the stage, at the other side of the room.

*

They sat at the table Elizabeth had claimed, sipping cocktails. Niamh attempted to demur as the waiter stood impatiently waiting for their order. In the end she bowed to Hubert's urgings to try something Latin and had left the choice to him. She was presented with a *Mojito Cubano*; an exotic mixture of light rum, crushed spearmint, fresh lime and sugar cane. Hubert stayed simple with a *Cuba Libre* (rum and coke with a squeeze of lime) and Elizabeth simplest of all with Jameson's neat.

The trio had years on the other patrons of the club. In fact, Niamh thought, she could be grandmother to one half and great-grandmother to the remainder. She took another swig of her drink.

Nothing for it but to go with the flow.

She made a decision.

She would try every cocktail on the menu and who knows, she might even get up to dance.

They ordered the second round and she and Hubert swapped: he had a *Mojito Cubano*, she a *Cuba Libre*. Elizabeth stayed with Jameson's.

The music was getting louder and louder: the room hotter and hotter. Elizabeth grabbed Hubert's hand and dragged him onto the dance floor into the swirling web of bodies. They created a space for themselves and, slowly, they started to feel the rhythm of the music, allowed their hips to sway and roll. The floor was too crowded for them to travel so they danced on the spot. They followed a quick succession of basic movements with a break step, establishing a connection that regulated their timing and the size of their steps, that built the arm tension necessary for particular steps to be led, until, finally, they were at one with each other and the music.

Niamh watched in astonishment, unable to believe that this was the same Hubert who found it difficult to keep pace with Elizabeth as she walked about the hotel. Perhaps Viagra invigorates the entire body not just ...

"Not bad, those oul ones, are they?" a young man who had taken Hubert's vacant seat, addressed Niamh.

"I'm afraid that's someone's seat," she said.

"I hate fuckin' Salsa," he said, his voice getting louder.

Niamh moved to Elizabeth's seat, but the disgruntled young man followed her along, occupying the chair she had just vacated. He hated Salsa because, apparently, his wife forced him to attend, what was for him, a weekly nightmare.

"Every Friday night I have to come to this hell-hole and me all done up like a ponce," he shouted. "She makes me wear black satin flares, a black satin shirt — with my belly — and Cuban-heeled boots. I swea' like a pig, me feet swell up like balloons and I can't get the feckin' boots off."

Niamh took a hefty swig of her drink and looked desperately to where she had last spotted Elizabeth and Hubert, but they had disappeared. The man lifted Hubert's glass to his lips, drank deeply from the *Mojito Cubano* and shuddered. "And she makes me drink this shite when all I want is a Guinness."

"I don't think that's your dri.." Niamh was cut off in mid-sentence.

The man launched into a long diatribe, this time about his appreciation of Salsa music: the interplay of the different instruments was, apparently, "fuckin' grea'," as was the high-pitched, hypnotic improvisation of the bongo against the bass of the conga: the amazing syncopation — the pushing and pulling when the musicians played off the beat. As for the stride piano! He took another deep swallow from the *Mojito Cubano*.

"The Latino music might be grea'," he said, "but their drinks are shite."

Still no sign of Elizabeth and Hubert and her cocktail almost finished and if she made a break for it tried to escape this madman she might never see them again but what the hell she could get a taxi back to the hotel and they would just have to worry about her not that that was likely they were well met those two only one thought between them and that was about sex.

The reluctant Salsa dancer was still talking. "As soon as we ge' here she drags me onto the floor. Every week. I feel such a prick. "You've got natural rhythm," she says. "You're just so ho'," she says, "all slippery and slidey in your satin. Let's show them what we can do, big boy," she says."

In desperation Niamh tried again. "Perhaps if you explained; if you told her how you feel, that dancing is not your thing …"

"I can't do tha'," he said, and Niamh was alarmed to hear the tears in his voice. Please god, she prayed silently, not a sobbing drunk.

"I can't do tha' — a promise is a promise — she loves Salsa, it's her whole life. She comes from the land of Salsa; has ended up in this fuckin' dump, where everything is cold and damp and where the last drop of passion has been squeezed from dance. I mean, for fuck sake, we pogo on the spot with our hands glued to our sides. I mean, nobody from Puerto Rica should have to settle for tha'."

At that moment her friends returned, glowing with sweat and pleasure. Without a word Elizabeth grabbed the young man's arm and pulled him onto the dance floor, motioning to Hubert to do the same with Niamh.

It was years since Niamh had danced — apart from a twirl round the house when, more and more rarely, she put her Elvis Presley vinyl onto the turntable and set the volume to maximum. She felt awkward and stiff as Hubert took hold of her right hand and placed his right hand on the small of her back.

"Relax," he said into her ear, "just feel the music. Left-right-left-pause right-left-right-pause," he shouted, leading her through the basic step. At first she stumbled and tripped, lost the beat, then something slotted into place; loud and clear she heard a clarion call from the past and her body responded to the insistent rhythm, the throbbing beat. Hips rolling, feet slipping easily over the polished floor, she followed Hubert's lead as he pulled her to him and with a slight flick of the wrist, pushed her away again. She twirled and spun as they rotated around one another, delighting in the controlled, simmering passion of Salsa.

*

Third time round Hubert ordered *Daiquiris* for both himself and Niamh and they sat flushed and exhausted, breathing heavily, sipping their drinks. Elizabeth and the young man danced their way to the table and flopped, completely spent, onto the vacant chairs.

"This is Seamus and he is a goer," Elizabeth laughed after she'd ordered a Jameson's for herself and a Guinness for him. "You can tell he's been taught by a native Latin American."

"Where is your wife?" Niamh asked, and as a look of anger mixed with pain flitted across Seamus' sweating face, immediately regretted it.

"She's dancing with tha' prick — mister slick ponce, the king of Salsa. Every week she makes me come here and every week she spends most of the evening twirling, slithering and sliding with *José* the poser from Puerto Rica, the greatest shite-hawk ..."

"Why do you put up with it?" Elizabeth butted in.

"I said to him, I said, do ya want yer teeth in a bag, but she got upset, so I didn't put a hand on him. Anyway, a promise is a promise — she's lonely; she's far away from home and he comes from her home town, so there's nothing …"

"Bullshite!" Elizabeth snapped. Seamus halted in mid-sentence, his eyes wide with surprise. "I'm sorry," Elizabeth continued, "but I can't listen to any more of this bullshite about immigrants. I've had enough of their sob-stories."

"If I might say," Niamh interrupted. But she was on to a loser. Elizabeth was on a roll.

"Don't we all have our personal narratives, most of which are liberally peppered with personal tragedies?" she said, her voice getting louder. "Those who are forced to, or choose to leave their own countries, too easily claim a monopoly on misery. Sure they never stop to consider what it's like to be the one who has to stay, the one who is stuck, having to shoulder the burden of keeping the show on the road while they're away discovering themselves, or a new land, or meeting new people with all the potential for danger, excitement and advancement this has to offer."

She stopped for breath and took a swig of her drink and Niamh tried once more to interject, but Elizabeth was off again. "And aren't the poor creatures who remain left to shoulder the stultifying responsibility of protecting and nurturing what emigrants sentimentally call the homeland? And don't those same emigrants feel free to be affronted if that homeland changes while they are away and don't they feel free to moan their heads off about the misery and hardship of life in exile — as though staying in some god-awful hell-hole was great for the spirit?"

Once again Elizabeth paused for breath and a large gulp of whiskey. Seamus kept his eyes lowered and then took a deep swig of his pint. He returned his glass to the table and a wisp of foam clung to his upper lip.

Hubert sipped his drink. He knew that the tiny woman he so admired had gone off on one, but unable to hear a word she said he remained unperturbed and simply marvelled at her oral energy.

Despite the fact that the music had stopped, a word here and a phrase there of Elizabeth's outpourings were lost in the din of other voices. Nevertheless, Niamh had heard enough by this stage to render her speechless. Elizabeth, she was sure, was on a sticky wicket. There were several points of her sweeping harangue that should be challenged and goodness knows she had tried.

But there were also points that touched a nerve that she would have to store up until she was somewhere quiet where she could consider and reflect on what had been said where she would try to decide to which part of the diatribe to give credence which part to reject.

*

A dark-haired woman, wearing a turquoise dress that clung to her generous curves, pushed her way through the packed dance floor, looking for her husband. She spotted Seamus and came quickly to claim him.

"Seamus," she said with a wide smile, "I have been looking everywhere for you, darling."

"Blind as well as dumb," Elizabeth muttered.

"I thought you were dancing with *José*," Seamus said, rather sourly.

"For me it was like being a little while at home," *Margareta's* full lips pouted sadly, "but now I must have the last dance with my wild Irish husband. Come on big boy," she said, her voice lowering to a whisper.

Give him his due, Seamus resisted for all of thirty seconds. Then he was on his feet, belly bulging and straining against the black satin of his shirt, feet screaming in agony inside his Cuban-heeled boots. He caught hold of *Margareta's* out-stretched hand and followed her onto the dance floor.

"There's one born every minute," Elizabeth said. She drained her glass and rose to her feet. "Right you two, time for bed." Niamh's jaw dropped in horror and Elizabeth gave her loud raucous laugh. "You've nothing to fear my prissy maid," she said, "I want this big boy all to myself. How about that then?"

At last she was out and about; had embarked on the final leg of her journey; was on her way to Rathmines.

That morning she had opened the curtains in her hotel room with some reluctance, fearing the weather would cut her off once again, but she needn't have worried. The sun sparkled and shone, turning the bay, which stretched from Dublin Port to Dun Laoghaire Pier, into a sheet of shimmering blue.

Directly opposite her window gulls had claimed a sandy hillock as their base and runway. Every few seconds a bird flew in swooping circles, skimming pools of gleaming water, before landing on the sand to become part of the dense, black mass already at rest: others flapped their wings and soared away, streaks of silver against the blue sky.

After several minutes Niamh turned away from the avian scene. She had much to do and she knew that she needed to use the time she had left in the city to the full. It was imperative that she made a start; did not allow herself to become entangled in any of Elizabeth's madcap schemes. As it was she was exhausted, aching in every bone in her body. The previous night she had used muscles she'd forgotten she possessed. Although Salsa was a sexy passionate dance, it required a great deal of muscle control, and exerting such control resulted in a high degree of discomfort.

*

She was fortunate. The number seven bus arrived just seconds after she reached the bus stop. She climbed the stairs (stiffly) and claimed a front seat from which she had an excellent view.

She loved this part of Dublin — the long straight thoroughfare of Merrion Road which led to Ballsbridge with its imposing buildings: the nineteenth century Masonic School — now a hotel — set well back from the road, its warm red brick glowing and welcoming in the morning sunshine: the sturdiness and grace of the grey stone Royal Dublin Society Headquarters, also nineteenth century, a symbol of colonial rule which endured and adapted — its nomenclature intact — in twenty-first century Dublin.

*

Despite their lack of money, Niamh, her mother and her siblings had enjoyed access, on more than one occasion, to this bastion of Anglo-Irish privilege.

Necessity, born of poverty, ensured that soldiers from the Irish army were only too willing to use their annual holidays and accept the casual work offered during the Spring Show and the Horse Show held at the RDS grounds. So, twice a year, with much connivance, the families of these soldiers joined the paying punters.

Niamh looked forward to these outings with mixed feelings. She enjoyed being able to swank at school about her trip to the RDS, but the reality was a jittery affair. On the appointed day her mother woke early, breakfasted with her husband, handed him his packed lunch and waved him off to work. Then she fed her brood, dressed them in their best attire, with strict instructions to sit quietly and not get dirty while she readied herself. Finally, the baby was handed over to the care of a neighbour and they were off.

There followed the long trek to the number eighteen bus stop and the equally long wait for the notoriously irregular bus to appear. All this time Niamh could sense her mother's unease — saw it in the set of her mouth, the anxious look in her grey eyes. When they arrived at Ballsbridge and crossed the road to the RDS, her mother's tension increased. Niamh and her brothers were given instructions they did not understand, but knew they must obey: they had to remain silent and, under no circumstances, salute their father or any neighbours they might see.

As they approached the large entrance her mother would hesitate, look around nervously, as though frightened she might be asked to leave. She then gathered her children close to her; gave them a warning glance and, regardless of length of queue, walked towards a particular turnstile that was invariably staffed by her husband or another man from Cathal Brugha Barracks. Without as much as a nod of recognition she requested six tickets and handed over a ten-shilling note. Had Niamh been vigilant she might have observed that the note was returned with the tickets and have understood how they could afford to patronize such a prestigious event and why her mother was a ragtaggle of nerves.

The Spring Show was her mother's favourite. Born and reared on a farm in the west of Ireland she loved the animals and the produce; and would spend annoying amounts of time gazing and touching while her children pulled at the leash, wanting to be off, running through the crowds, playing hide and seek, getting lost, whinging for ice-cream.

Although gaining entry to the show-jumping competitions added another layer of anxiety to the day, Niamh's preference was for the Horse Show that took place in August. Once inside the main entrance they would skirt the grounds, trying to spot a familiar face on duty at one of the many entrances to the arena, mount the steep stairs, hand over non-existing tickets and take a seat while remaining ever-ready to move in case those who had genuinely booked the places should appear.

From this precarious vantage point Niamh could observe the magic of show-jumping — the powerful horses, groomed to shining perfection as they galloped round the arena, responding to their riders' bidding, soaring over fences and negotiating obstacles. She loved it all; watched with rapt attention; breathed in the horsy smell; was entranced by the pounding hooves which beat out a rhythm that seemed to stir some primitive longing.

And then they would have to move, pretend they had mistakenly sat in the wrong place, hunt for another batch of seats; ignore their kindly neighbour on the way out.

There was one more treat before they started the long trek home. They would go in search of the bandstand and listen to the Number One Army Band, something they did every day. But this was different: the men were resplendent in full dress uniform, their brass instruments gleamed in the sun and hundreds of strangers sat and listened with rapt attention to what people in the barracks took for granted. Listening to the wonderful music that soared above the enraptured crowds made Niamh and her family feel proprietorial and smug.

As the light began to fade they waited with hundreds more for a bus that never came, repeated the long trek from bus stop to home, fell wearily and crankily into bed.

Despite the difficulties, the anxieties that the adults had to endure to achieve their day out, the feeling persisted that they had, indeed, achieved something special. For once the likes of them had sampled something intended for others: and they had done it by sticking together. They had used their collective muscle to outwit their betters and it felt good.

*

Heavy traffic forced the bus to a halt outside the American Embassy on the corner of Pembroke Road. Although much lauded (by those who purported to know about such things) for the imagination and skill of its designers in combining modern materials with features found in fifth century Celtic monuments, Niamh and many of her fellow Dubliners disliked the circular building, took against it from the outset, saw in the pre-cast concrete modular units of its construction a crude belligerence.

That was back in the sixties when the building had been completed. As Niamh looked at it now she thought how well the rough, circular edifice with its unseeing windows, reflected the unheeding and apparently limitless power of the country it represented. The fact that two floors of the embassy were below ground had always given her the creeps, elicited dark thoughts she had no wish to explore.

Thinking of America brought W.B. to mind. He had sent another email, asking if she had received the essays on Joyce he had posted. He had added a postscript, urging her to come to New York, to come before winter set in so that she and his grandmother might stroll through Central Park together, visit The Metropolitan Museum, have tea at the Algonquin Hotel.

Niamh was touched by W.B.'s persistence, by his naïve hope that a stranger could make a difference to his grandmother's final months.

But Niamh did not want to visit New York.

She imagined it one of loneliest places on earth.

*

She disembarked from the bus in Westmoreland Street, wanting to saunter across O'Connell Bridge and soak up the atmosphere of the bustling city. As she made her way through the crowd she spotted a familiar face. It was her niece. Niamh smiled joyfully; she raised her hand and waved, calling her niece's name. The young woman looked at her without recognition and disappeared into the dense throng.

Only to be expected hadn't seen her family for years just the occasional phone call so her niece wouldn't have a clue what she looked like what with the curly ginger hair having turned into a mesh of beige the slim figure encased in a generous layer of blubber and she only recognized the young woman because she was the spit of Paul anyway her family had never been interested in her life outside Dublin which was ninety-nine-point-nine-nine-nine-per-cent of her existence so no point.

Most of her life she had clung like a barnacle to relationships long dead: saw only waste and loss when indifference replaced love. But recently she had changed her view, had come to accept that though people move on, lose contact, they are not lost to us. The people who touch us deeply remain with us to the end, are part of the muscle and sinew of our being, have helped make us who we are.

She lowered the arm she had raised in futile salutation and hurried across the road to catch the number fourteen bus. She would take the bus to the Town Hall, call into Rathmines Library where she had spent many hours as a child scouring the shelves for Enid Blyton's books. She had loved *The Secret Seven* and *The Famous Five* series, envied the comfortable and adventure-filled lives of the boys and girls who peopled the books, envied their midnight feasts when they munched on juicy apples and smooth chocolate.

She would stroll up Leinster Road; take a right into Erin Terrace and into what remained of Cathal Brugha Barracks.

She had pushed through the great doors of the library, was climbing the wide stairs to the first floor when her mobile phone rang. By the time she had fumbled in her handbag and located it, the ringing had stopped. She looked at the screen and discovered that she had missed three calls. Scrolling down and viewing last numbers, she saw that Elizabeth had been the caller. Ah feck it, she thought; I need to get on with what I'm doing; Elizabeth and her crackpot ideas will have to wait.

She was ensconced in the reference library, a copy of Homer's *Odyssey* lying on the table in front of her, glancing, occasionally, out of the open window at the nearby Town Hall. The clock was chiming the half hour when she heard her text-message ring-tone. The other readers looked at her with disdain as she hurried from the room, struggling to find the noisy instrument.

"Please contact now. URGENT," Elizabeth had written.

I'm on roaming so it will cost a small fortune for me to ring her, was Niamh's first thought. She switched the phone to silent, turned on her heel and headed for the reference library. As she pushed the heavy door open she felt her phone vibrate. It was Elizabeth again. A shiver of anxiety ran through Niamh as she pressed the green button and held the phone to her ear.

"Please come back immediately. Please come back now," Elizabeth said, and her voice collapsed in a sob.

The sexual mores of the residents of Cathal Brugha Barracks were, undoubtedly, no different from those of the rest of the population, but the insularity of the community seemed to tighten the stranglehold exerted by the catholic church over such matters, resulting in rather strange goings-on.

Although evidence of sexual activity abounded in 1950s Ireland (most families were large) sex was not spoken of except as a subject of lewd comment and dirty jokes. The catholic church's line on the subject was clear; sex was permissible within the holy sacrament of marriage: period. Sexual pleasure was not countenanced; the function of the sex act was to procreate, to bring other catholics into the world. Intercourse outside marriage was a mortal sin. But the matter didn't end there: a sexual thought, a kiss, a fumble were sins as well, so catholics lived their lives in a constant state of siege, cut off from the pleasures of a natural act by guilt and fear. Both men and woman suffered as a result, but women carried an additional burden: should they (even unwittingly) by any action or word cause a man to be sexually aroused or to have impure thoughts, their souls would be blighted by yet another sin.

*

Like all young children Niamh experienced sexual pleasure without being aware of what it was; warm twinges, fleeting lances of pleasing sensation deep within her young body left her excited and unsettled. Like all young children she observed behaviour and rituals that she could not make sense of, found vaguely disturbing. Her first kiss, a light touch of soft lips on her unsuspecting mouth, stolen from her when she was seven by her godmother's nephew, awakened feelings of agitation and longing.

It was at this time also that she first witnessed the mating ritual of the Band Boys and the pubescent girls from married quarters, sensed the barely suppressed charge of this encounter, was excited and unsettled by it, though many years would pass before she understood the reason for her disquiet.

*

The Number One Army Band did not add just music to the ambiance of the barracks: it also added a sexual imperative, an urgency for each successive generation that would not be denied, whatever the teachings of the catholic church.

Army School of Music trainees were required to follow a strict regime: they ate at set times, attended classes throughout the day, played sport and retired at nine o'clock each evening. But this rigid schedule did little to quieten their leppin' hormones, nor could it keep the Band Boys and the girls apart. Lust will find a way.

Irish soldiers were not highly esteemed by the people they served. The reasons for this were complex and probably had their roots in the tragedy of the civil war, but it was a truth universally acknowledged that soldiers did not enjoy a high social standing, and a fact left unsaid that military folk accepted this degrading estimation of their own worth. Spoken or not, facts will out. And they did. Ordinary soldiers were not considered a good catch for young women whose fathers were ordinary soldiers. But Band Boys were a different matter entirely; they were prime meat, their musical talent lending them a special aura. The young women of the barracks chased them indefatigably and the chase started early.

It was a summer evening during the school holidays when Niamh first witnessed the chase in progress. All the mothers of A and B Blocks were sitting outside their front doors and all the children were pushing themselves towards exhaustion, shouting, laughing, skipping, playing relievio, broken statues, piggy beds, marbles, rounders or simply running frantically in all directions. Into this cauldron of activity came a group of teenage girls skipping, giggling and preening. The skirts of their poplin dresses bobbed and swirled, a rainbow of bright colours, as they progressed towards the stairs of A Block.

"We all know what they're after," Mrs. Cassidy said.

"Let's hope they don't get more than they bargained for," Mrs. Brady gave a chesty laugh.

"He'd want to have a fantastic aim, not to mention a gigantic …"

"Niamh, how many times do I have to tell you not to stand where adults are talking," her mother's voice cut in, and Niamh felt a steely grip on her arm. "Go and play with Kay," she said, and pushed her daughter away from the laughing women.

Niamh ignored her mother's command and trailed the giggling teenagers around the corner where they climbed to the top of the stairs and stood on the veranda. She watched in puzzled silence as they hung out of the railings, slid down the banisters, shouted and squealed. They pushed each other, ran down the stairs and up again. Every time they reached the top they looked towards a building on the other side of the towering wall that separated married quarters from down the barracks and, apparently ignorant of, or indifferent to the church's teaching about arousing young men, they waved crazily and began singing the provocative lyrics of *Music! Music! Music!*

Niamh felt a tug on her arm. "I thought I told you to play with Kay," her mother said. "You can go in now for being bold. In, I said, this minute." As Niamh slinged towards her front door she heard her mother address the young women.

"Go home out of that and don't be making a show of yourselves," she said. "Have ye no shame, at all? Flaunting yourselves and singing a song that ye know very well has been banned by the church."

*

Catholic teaching did not have the last word on sexual practices, however. Pleasure and attitudes may have been tainted and distorted by the church's bile, but the strength of the sexual urge meant that many of the faithful were willing to be unfaithful, to flout catholic dogma. Tommy Doherty had risked all for the sake of a roll in the hay with the bold Francie. And he wasn't the only man in the barracks to transgress. Bill Carey was known to be an energetic philanderer. Less understandably, at a time when intercourse almost inevitably resulted in pregnancy, some women also sought satisfaction outside of marriage.

These violations, though frowned upon, were tolerated. Every adult knew what was going on, but they kept their lips buttoned, offered up a prayer for the sinners, hoped fervently that they or their spouses would not be tempted.

But some practices were less easily ignored, although the good folk of the barracks did their best to do so. Incidents of incest were suspected, but went unchallenged. And it was known that the daughters of one family were encouraged to, and actually did, join their mother on the game, plying their trade around Baggot Street. Again, nothing was done.

And then there was the peeping tom.

He appeared in the early sixties and Niamh was one of his first victims.

The flats in married quarters were without bathrooms. A communal bathhouse had been built in the late 1950s, but was opened during daylight hours only, six days a week; consequently, working adults were forced to wash at the kitchen sink.

It was a Tuesday evening and, as usual, Niamh had the ground floor flat to herself. It was her night for washing. First she washed her clothes; then she stripped to her bra and pants and shampooed her hair, after which she removed her underwear and gave herself a full body wash. She donned her nightdress and dressing gown, arranged her hair in large curlers, lifted the heavy basin of washing and walked to the bedroom next to the kitchen. She opened the sash window, steadied the basin on the sill, climbed onto the sill and prepared to jump into the misty twilight to get to the clothesline. A flurry of movement stopped her in her tracks. A figure jumped from the kitchen windowsill and scarpered into the encroaching darkness.

*

"Are you sure you didn't imagine it?" her mother asked over and over, unwilling to accept the significance of what her daughter said. "You know your sight is not the best and as you said yourself, wasn't it nearly dark?"

"Leave her alone, Grainne," her father commanded quietly. "If she said she saw someone then it must be true. Don't worry *a leanbh,*" he assured Niamh, "we'll put a stop to this."

When, five years later, Niamh left Ireland for good, the peeping tom was still terrorizing the women of the barracks. Everyone knew who it was; many swore they had seen him clearly; Niamh's eldest brother had chased him off on one occasion. Although a good runner he had not actually caught the culprit, but he had seen him clearly enough to identify him. But nothing was done. No one was willing to confront the gentle mother and strict father with the truth of their son's disturbing behaviour. Despite the evidence of their own children no adult really accepted that a young man from a good catholic family spent his evenings peeping through curtains at their naked daughters.

At no point did the community think to involve the police, civilian or military. The reasons for this were not straightforward. In theory, the *Garda Siochana* had jurisdiction over residents of married quarters, the

Military Police over indiscretions of military personnel on military property, but the fact that military personnel lived with their civilian families within the compound complicated matters. In practice, the *Garda Siochana* kept well away and the residents wanted to keep it that way. What happened in married quarters was the concern of the people in married quarters. They would sort it themselves. In its way it was a grand sentiment. The only problem was, it didn't work.

In the end it was Niamh's younger brother who pushed her father into doing the deed. Her brother spotted the *voyeur* as he stood on a windowsill in broad daylight, peeping into his mother's room. Her brother made it clear that if something was not done to put a stop to the young man's activities he and his friends would make sure that the pervert would find it impossible to climb onto any windowsill with two broken legs. Niamh's father imparted the information to the young man's father, who in turn accused Mr. O' Riordan of a terrible calumny.

But from then on the women of the barracks found that they could wash in peace, free from the fear of being spied on by a pair of fervid eyes through a slit in the curtains.

*

When the men of the barracks went on their first major tour of duty for the United Nations in 1960 another menace appeared. Many families were left without their men-folk and these families were terrorized by a nocturnal caller who, keeping to the shadows, crept along, rattled door handles and, in a hoarse whisper, demanded to be allowed in, assuring the terrified woman within that he would dispel the sexual frustration she was undoubtedly feeling in the absence of her husband. Again the identity of the villain was soon known and again he went unchallenged. These things did not happen in catholic Ireland and, anyway, wouldn't it be a terrible blow to his wife and family to learn that they had a pervert for a husband and father?

*

But attitudes gradually changed. In England the sixties were in full swing and notions that women were equal to men drifted over the water and many women in Ireland welcomed them warmly. And besides, the women of the barracks had had enough. When the next prowler came on the scene in the late nineteen sixties they demanded that the men set up a vigilante group to catch him in the act. If the men didn't do it, by the Lord Harry, the women themselves would.

The vigilantes brought their mission to a successful conclusion, but not before both Niamh and her father almost died of fright.

On holiday from Birmingham and unaware of the activities of the nascent organization, Niamh had visited a friend in G Block and was sauntering home along the boundary of the field when she heard a movement in the long grass within inches of where she walked. Looking to her left, she spotted a man crawling on all fours. The moon shone on his blackened face and his eyes were luminous orbs in the dark. She let out a scream and, with heart pounding as though it would burst, raced for the safety of home.

The next night her father, thinking to do his bit to protect the fair sex, decided to patrol the immediate area round his home. As was his wont he walked, head down and hands clasped behind his back. He rounded the corner at the end of the block and strode out across the rough grass, heading towards the rear of his flat where his wife and daughter were preparing for bed.

He had passed the narrow path that led to B Block when it happened. A hoarse shout rent the air, "I've got you, you bastard," the voice declaimed, "And then," her father later explained, "the stupid eejit nearly decapitated me with a hurley stick, although why Brendan O'Farrell would chose a hurley stick for a weapon is beyond me. Sure he was always useless at the game."

The prowler was not named and shamed. It was thought to be unnecessary. No doubt fearful for his life, he abandoned his nocturnal activities and the women of the barracks slept easily in their beds once again, at risk only from the overtures of over-zealous husbands.

The taxi pulled up outside the hotel and Elizabeth ran immediately to meet it.

"What kept you? Did you come via Kerry? You've been ages."

"I came as soon as I could. The traffic was dreadful." Niamh climbed from the vehicle, paid the driver and walked towards the bar entrance.

"Where do you think you're going?" Elizabeth asked.

"I could murder a cup of tea. I'm parched."

Elizabeth lowered her voice. "There's no time for that," she said, in a savage whisper, "this is serious."

The deep furrows on Elizabeth's face seemed to have unfurled and the skin sagged and drooped with weariness; her usually taunting eyes were blank and pale. Without a word Niamh followed her through the main door, across the foyer and into the lift.

When the key turned in the lock of Elizabeth's room door she opened it a fraction, pushed Niamh through the narrow slit, followed her quickly, checking that the do not disturb sign was still in place, and shut the door quietly.

The curtains were closed, shutting out all light and the sea view. Niamh stood still, trying to get her bearings.

"Why are we in the dark?" she asked after a few moments.

"That's why." Elizabeth pointed to the bed.

"If you think for one minute that I'm getting involved in your hanky-panky …"

Elizabeth cut her off. "Look," she said, "just look," her voice a strangled sob.

Niamh walked closer to the bed and then stopped. A long narrow shape bulged beneath the bedclothes. She looked from the bed to Elizabeth and back again to the bed.

"What is it?"

"It's not a what."

"What do you mean?"

"It's a he."

"If it's not a stupid question, why is he in your bed? Why doesn't he get up?"

"He can't."

"If you don't want to know the answer, don't ask the question," her mother had often said.

But Niamh asked it anyway.

"What's going on?"

*

With a quick glance at the shape in the bed Elizabeth took Niamh's hand and pulled her towards the chairs by the window. When they were seated she recounted the whole sorry saga.

The previous night, when she and Hubert had left Niamh, they had rushed to this room flushed with excitement from their passionate night of Salsa and, with the aid of the magical pill, had enjoyed uninhibited sex that went on for ages and ages. When she woke the next morning she was knackered, but Hubert was still up for it — literally. Not wanting to disappoint him and always chary of refusing something that might never be on offer again, Elizabeth agreed.

"And sure then it happened." She looked at Niamh and tears welled in her eyes and streamed down her wrinkled cheeks.

"What, what happened?"

"He took a great gulp of air, emitted a moan which I took for a cry of ecstasy and collapsed on top of me."

"And?"

"I tried to push him off, but he was too heavy."

"Why didn't you ask him to get off?"

"Of course I asked him but…"

"Well, I know he's as deaf as a post, but surely you could make him …"

"Are you a complete omodon? He couldn't hear because … because …" Elizabeth let out a searing sob. "He couldn't hear because he's dead. Didn't it take me ages to get out from under him," she ended flatly.

Niamh felt queasy. She was sure the walls of the room moved slightly and that the ceiling swayed. Her mind skeetered away from the reality of what she had just been told and led her to the banal realization that life is full of surprises, that even at her age it was possible to experience something for the first time, that for the last fifteen minutes she had been sitting close to the body of a man who had committed sex suicide.

*

She managed to usher Elizabeth out the door, along the corridor and into her own sun-drenched room. She led her friend to the chair by the window, went into the bathroom, returned with two glasses and poured generous measures from the remains of the bottle of whiskey Elizabeth had left after their drunken binge a few nights previously.

Niamh sat on the edge of the bed nearest the window, sipping her drink, comforted by the warm sensation of the golden liquid as it trickled and spread from her chest to her stomach. There were many questions she needed to ask, but she was playing for time, knowing that the information she received would demand action that would, in turn, lead to more action which, she was sure, would not be pleasant.

When she glanced at Elizabeth she saw that she was gazing out at the wide sweep of Dublin Bay with unseeing eyes. The incoming tide approached at a leisurely pace; tiny wavelets, capped with curls of white, broke gently onto the great stretch of sand. The afternoon was still and serene as though holding its breadth.

*

"Have you told anyone?" Niamh asked, knowing the answer.

"No, of course not."

"Why not?"

"If this gets out my reputation will be in shreds."

"Your reputation for what?"

Elizabeth kept her unseeing eyes glued to the scene beyond the window.

"My reputation as a highly respected academic."

"But you despise all that. You said yourself that the academic life is a charade, that most academic writing and conferences are aimed at small cliques and have little relationship to the wider world."

"Yes, but it's my world; it's all I have; I've devoted my life to it."

*

They sat on for some time, gazing out the window at the sun-soaked scene as the tide continued its inexorable advance. At last Niamh raised herself from the bed. She walked to where Elizabeth was sitting and placed her hand, gently, on the woman's shoulder.

"It's time," she said. "We should let the hotel manager know what happened. We should attend to Hubert."

"But what about his reputation?" Elizabeth looked pleadingly at Niamh. "He was a highly respected, evolutionary biologist: world renowned," she finished with a sob.

"We'll make sure that this will add to his reputation," Niamh said. "We can maintain that he died in the interests of science, testing the thesis that man has evolved sufficiently to push the boundaries of sexual activity way past what Shakespeare could have imagined when he outlined his seven ages of man. How about that then?"

*

When they divulged their secret they nearly had another fatality on their hands. The hotel manager's eyes popped and bulged as Niamh told him that a dead man lay upstairs in his hotel, that he had been there for about twelve hours and that he had died in the room of a female guest.

"Little gurriers," he said, wiping the sweat from his brow with a large handkerchief. "The youth of today can't leave it alone; at it like rabbits, morning, noon and night and the little bastards have to die in my hotel, causing no end of trouble. If the press gets hold of this I'm finished."

The knowledge that it was not a young man who had died but an eminent scientist of advanced years did nothing to assuage the manager's anxiety.

There followed a round of interviews with the police. No, Elizabeth could not remove her belongings from the room until cause of death had been established and all forensic tests completed. She must remain close at hand for further questioning. She was lucky she was not taken into custody. The deliberate non-disclosure of a death for a period of twelve hours was a serious matter.

The hotel manager offered her another room, but the previously formidable woman had (temporarily Niamh hoped) lost her spunk. So, rather reluctantly, it must be said, Niamh invited her to share her room.

As she alighted at the nearest bus stop to Leinster Road the Town Hall clock struck the hour. She crossed at the pedestrian crossing and made her way up the long thoroughfare. To her right, the large house once owned by their family doctor was enclosed behind a high fence, suggesting that those who lived there had something terrible to hide or something very precious to protect. Given the wealth the old miser had accumulated serving the sick; it was probably the latter, Niamh thought. "That fella is so greedy he'd take the eye out of your head and come back for the eyelashes" was a remark regularly made of the good doctor.

As a child she had been shy of the stout man who, very occasionally, bustled into her home dressed in an expensive navy suit and snowy white shirt, clasping a shiny bag from which he pulled shiny instruments.

She sensed that her mother was in awe of the fat man who was always in a hurry. In his presence her confidence and authority evaporated. She would speak to him nervously, listen attentively to what he said, thank him profusely for his advice, for coming at her bidding, hand him seven shillings and six pence (a huge sum for her mother to pay) and see him to the door, all the while offering her heartfelt thanks.

Further along on the left-hand side, opposite the row of Georgian houses that lined the road, a group of chestnut and lime trees stood tall and proud. In the bright sunshine of an autumn day it was easy to admire the strength and girth of these fine specimens, to feel a glow of pleasure at the dense clusters of golden leaves that crowned each tree, but Niamh knew that on winter evenings their broad trunks afforded an effective screen for men whose purpose it was to get off on frightening women. The memory of the local flasher jumping from behind a tree, his white face framed by a straggly beard, holding his penis proudly in one hand and rubbing it frantically with the other, still had the power to make her cringe with revulsion.

She hurried on past the Nun's Lane, not wishing to dwell on the time she had spent at the school that lurked there. Further along she noticed that Dalton School no longer existed — the fine Georgian house still stood proudly with it counterparts on either side — but the school had gone and with it the Prof, the tiny man who had amused them endlessly with his extravagant movements, his resplendent moustache, his over-sized cap and gown. He was like no one else they had known and, as is the way with children, they were cruel and nasty to him, shouting abuse from a safe distance. But he took it all with a smile and a wave of the hand, eventually winning the war of attrition because the children learned that there is no fun to be had insulting someone who won't play the game, who refuses to be insulted.

The lettering on the two stone pillars that guarded the opening of Erin Terrace was faint and worn with age. Niamh hesitated for a moment, remembering the thousands of times she had entered this narrow lane that opened out at the other end into the large compound of Cathal Brugha Barracks. Invariably, after the long trek up Leinster Road, she would arrive at this point in her journey, weary and exhausted, but the sight of the stone pillars spurred her on. She would pick up speed and run the final yards home.

She couldn't imagine that she would ever pass this way again so she stood awhile looking right and left. She was equidistant between Harold's Cross Road and Rathmines Road and if she spanned out a mile north and south from this point she would cover the boundaries of her childhood — give or take the occasions when she went to Sandymount or Stephen's Green with her mother or to the Dodder River with her brothers.

Over the past eleven days she had traversed most of her childhood territory. All that remained was to visit the place that had been the centre of her world as she grew to maturity in her native city.

*

The great iron-gate that had once guarded the married quarters had gone. A red brick wall inscribed with the words Grosvenor Lodge stood to the left of where it had once been.

Niamh advanced, slowly, trying to get her bearings. The seven blocks of flats that had been built in the nineteenth century to house British soldiers and that had, subsequently, been home to hundreds of Irish families, were gone, replaced by three rows of sturdy neo-Georgian terraces, one to her left and, she saw in the distance, two more bordering the military compound. To her right a line of neat redbrick houses squatted; tucked into a corner further along was a cluster of buildings she could not quite see from her present position.

The field where she had played as a child had survived, dominated by goal posts for Gaelic games, although if the waist-high grass was anything to go by, it was some time since anyone had kicked a ball or swung a hurley-stick on that patch of green. And something else that was new: berries hung in scarlet clusters from the rowan trees that braided the field. Niamh felt sure she would have remembered such brilliance had it been a constant during her early years. In her mind's eye she saw huge chestnut and sycamore trees.

She followed the road to her right, past the row of squat dwellings and now had a clear view of the houses built where she imagined D Block had once stood. In stark contrast to the other buildings on site, a clutch of dingy houses huddled together as though shamed by their shabbiness. The pebbledash exteriors were painted, in the words of Joyce, snot-green; a tracery of cracks spread across the ugly facades. Some premonition told her that these were the new army houses, the homes built after the demolition of A B C D E F G blocks, the homes thought fit for the families of twenty-first century Irish soldiers.

*

Overcome by a wave of fatigue she flopped onto the kerb of one of the grassy islands dotted strategically to control traffic-flow. As she sat she became aware of the sound of silence: an all-pervasive unnatural quiet — no voices, no traffic — nothing.

She closed her eyes, allowed herself to let go, to float back in time. The dense silence gradually dissipated and was filled with the noise of children laughing shouting crying the trundle of fuel carts delivering coal turf and logs to each home the steady clip-clop of horses' hooves music soaring from the band-room church bells calling the faithful to mass the voices of neighbours singing children chanting skipping rhymes adult voices raised in anger and more rarely in joy the sound of a slap followed by a wail of anguish the striking of the Town Hall clock the thwack of a skipping rope the bouncing of a ball the ecstatic roar of the crowd as her brother led Ireland to victory against Portugal her mother's voice calling her home.

In her mind's eye she saw all the people who had made her world. Her mother small and slim a beauty with black hair and clear grey eyes her father the living embodiment of the cliché tall dark and handsome the rock on which her childhood was built her demon brothers quick agile sometimes cruel always ready to defend her against outsiders small rotund Marie her first loss Cathleen Byrne waxen and still tall skinny Philomena blamed unfairly for leading her astray the constant flow of men in uniform drifting backwards and forwards the green river around which the tributaries of the barracks its women and children rippled and swirled an officer flanked by his aides inspecting each flat to ensure that forbidden electrical appliances wirelesses electric fires or irons were not used her mother's rush to find a hiding place for the offending article when the alarm went up that he was on his way Mrs. McGillicuddy foaming frothing away in the head Tommy Doherty's passion wagon gleaming in the evening sun a gang of jeering children running after it as far as the Cross Gate Seamus Deane *scuttin'* a lorry as it raced towards the canteen to deliver provisions Mrs. Maguire's anguished screams a ribbon of black hard-packed ice stretching the length of F Block her future husband staggering in the dark losing his footing sliding on his backside along its length Mr. Reilly playing his accordion his eyes wild with delight neighbours she had known all her life squealing with admiration at the sight of her wedding gown shouting encouragement and farewell as she left home and Ireland for good.

Image crowded image, flitting, overlapping, rewinding, fast-forwarding — a film of her life wound and rewound by a crazed projectionist.

Interspersed with the sounds and sights were the smells. She took a deep breath and her nostrils were filled with the rich primitive smell of turf burning of bread baking the sweet-sour tang of apples that had escaped their covering of pastry and bubbled and blistered on the plate the pong of her brothers' sweaty feet the intoxicating smell of the polish her father worked into his belt boots and leggings the stink of the abattoir that wafted into the barracks on slaughter day the sharp clean odour of Dettol used extravagantly after the birth of each baby but at no other time the heavy aroma of stout that frequently battled with the clean soapy smell of her father.

But it was her mother's smell that was most palpable, most manifest, which was peculiar, because her mother smelled of no single substance. Her mother's smell was milky, musty, tangy, earthy. She smelt of the foods she cooked throughout the day, of the soaps and powders she used to clean the flat, wash the clothes and her children. She smelt of the sweat she spent while carrying out the heavy burden of tasks that filled her days and sometimes her nights as well. Her smell was tantalizingly familiar, yet contained a hint of something beyond knowing.

As she sat on the grassy island, in the autumn sunshine, Niamh finally solved the mystery of that most familiar of smells; recognized not just the essence of her mother in it but her own essence as well.

*

She opened her eyes, looked around into the quiet space.

Not a sinner to be seen.

Not a sound to be heard.

With a hand either side of her rump she pushed herself into a standing position, stood stiffly for a moment to steady herself before walking in the direction of the Cross Gate.

The gate had been locked into place by metal bolts, cutting off access between married quarters and the military section of the barracks. The hut that had stood in the military section and which her father had frequently manned, had been knocked down, but the band-room was still *in situ,* as was the sergeants' mess.

At last she spotted another human being. Through the open window of the mess she saw a young soldier, playing a leisurely game of billiards, something she had seen her father do many times in that very room. The young man was strong and tanned and, from time to time, he stopped playing and addressed someone Niamh could not see.

She turned and retraced her steps. As far as she could tell the military section of the compound was as she remembered it, but she couldn't square this perception with the feeling that the space where married quarters had once been had shrunk. Try as she may she could not fit the seven blocks of flats and the land that had surrounded them into the existing area.

Once again she walked past the army houses. A lone boy negotiated his scooter to the rear of a line of parked cars. He looked up as Niamh passed, but without curiosity, lost in a world of his own.

The heavy silence was broken, suddenly, by the clatter of conversation. Niamh turned and saw four adults emerge from a neo-Georgian house. They waved their arms about, spoke in the loud expressive tones of southern Europe, hugged and kissed each other as though in farewell, linked arms and walked off, still talking and laughing loudly.

A flicker of movement caught her eye as she passed the first of the sickly-green houses and on impulse she walked up the path and spoke to the woman who emerged from the shadows of the hallway.

"Good afternoon," Niamh said, "I wonder if you could tell me how old these houses are?" The woman stared at her blankly for a few seconds. When she raised her hand to push a wisp of blonde hair from her eyes it seemed to take a great effort.

"My husband is not here," she said.

Niamh repeated her question. "I wonder if you would know how old these houses are?"

The woman plucked at her blouse with agitated fingers, looked beyond Niamh's head as though hoping someone would appear.

"I used to live in the barracks." Niamh said, "Many years ago I lived in the barracks and I was wondering when these houses were built."

"You don't have an Irish accent." The woman smiled a satisfied smile as though she had uncovered a plot.

"I've lived away a long time."

"My husband and me, we talk about things a lot. When he's here. But he's not always here."

Niamh smiled and turned to go. "The houses, they were built twenty-six years ago. We've put in for a transfer lots and lots of times, but we have no children so they always turn us down."

The two women sat drinking coffee in the foyer of the hotel. They had dined together, Niamh on sea bass, broccoli and boiled potatoes, Elizabeth on her usual coddle, and had filled each other in on the day's events.

The respected academic had recovered somewhat from the travails of the previous day. The sleeping pill, which Niamh had given her, combined with a few shots of the hard stuff, had knocked her out and she had slept well into the morning, missed breakfast, took a walk to Blackrock; through the park and back again. The police had interviewed her — going over the same rigmarole again and again, insinuating that she was not as innocent as she made out. She'd never claimed to be innocent for Christ's sake. She was a worldly woman, that's why she was in the mess she was in, but to think that she might be implicated in Hubert's death showed a stupidity that was worrying in the national police who were supposed to solve crime and protect citizens. Sure there was no motive. It was in her interests to keep Hubert alive. Didn't the stupid little buggers realize how difficult it was for a woman of her age to find a sexual partner who was capable of raising himself off a chair let alone raising his …

"I get the picture," Niamh cut in, "but surely they must have finished with you by now."

"Well I'm free to leave the hotel, to return home, provided I surrender my passport and don't attempt to leave the country. Apparently, it will take weeks before the forensic tests are completed."

"I've got an idea," Niamh said.

"Yes?"

"Let's get *rilo,* absolutely *stotious.*"

"I might agree if I knew what the hell you were talking about."

"Call yourself an Irishwomen? If you want it in plain English — let's get plastered."

*

They adjourned to the bar and ordered a bottle of Irish. Taking Niamh at her word, Elizabeth poured a large measure and knocked it back in one deep swallow. Despite her earlier bravado Niamh's approach was more circumspect. She sipped the smooth mellow liquid, enjoyed the soothing warmth that spread from her throat to her chest.

"Have you heard anything from that young American you were so smitten with?"

"Yes," Niamh said, refusing to rise to her friend's gibe. "Yes, as a matter of fact I have. He wants me to visit New York."

"Aren't you the dark horse?" Elizabeth jerked upright. "You've got yourself a toy boy."

"Will you ever grow up? He wants me to meet his terminally ill Irish grandmother, talk to her about home, and take her to her favourite places in The Big Apple before she dies."

"Sounds right up your street."

"I'm not going,"

Elizabeth opened her mouth to deliver another quip, but the sharpness of Niamh's tone stopped her and instead she helped herself to another generous measure of *uisce baithe.*

*

Another email had awaited her when she'd returned to the hotel the previous evening. W.B. had adopted a teasing tone. "I'm sorry to burst a bubble for you, Aunty Niamh, but your romantic notion of sitting in Bewley's, reading Joyce's masterpiece and imagining him quaffing coffee in the self same spot many years before is, as we say in these parts, so much boloney. The great man had left Dublin for good before the restaurant opened in 1927." But desperation had crept in at the end. 'When are you going back to Birmingham? Grandma would love to see you soon. Just say the word and I'll book a direct flight to New York." And he had ended the message with the simple plea, "Please come."

She was moved by the young man's plight; touched by his deep affection for his grandmother, but she could not do as he asked. She had never been to New York, was unnerved by the very idea of the city. Hovering on the fringes of her memory were the images of the place conjured by her mother's repeated stories of how her aunts and uncles had battled to survive its concrete jungle, of the place where her young cousin had burnt to death in a furnace. These images were augmented by the portrayal of the city in the many films and television programmes she had seen set against its brutal backdrop. New York was imprinted on her imagination as a place where loneliness was etched in every face, carved into the very bones of the city.

So she would not go.

W.B.'s grandmother would have to manage without her.

"I went to the pictures tomorrow.
I got a front seat in the back.
I fell from the pit to the gallery
And broke a front bone in my back.
A woman, she gave me some sweets,
I ate them and gave them back."

Niamh repeated the rhyme over and over to the rhythm of the DART as it trundled, unhurriedly, between Dun Laoghaire and Sandycove station.

It was her last full day in Dublin and she was making her last call. Elizabeth sat opposite, looking with unseeing eyes at the watery landscape. The sound of foreign voices, predominantly Polish, (as far as Niamh could tell) hissed and clattered round the carriage.

Elizabeth roused herself. "What's that rubbish you're spouting?" she asked.

"It's a ditty we used to say as kids, when we went to the pictures, but I don't think I've got it right. I think I'm missing a few lines."

"The literary world will be the poorer for it."

"Speaking of the literary, how significant do you think dramatic tension is in *Ulysses*?

"I think it would be fair to say that the book is replete with tension between the inner and outer worlds."

"So you wouldn't agree that dramatic tension is the real curse of the novel form?"

"In what sense do you mean a curse?"

"I'm trying to decide whether there is any truth in Kundera's claim that in subordinating every aspect of the novel to the drive towards dramatic tension the form is stripped of the beautiful, the surprising, the philosophical and is, consequently, the poorer for it."

"I think you are asking two different questions, but it's too early in the day to tackle matters of such import. I'll get back to you when I've had a few."

When the train slid to a halt, they disembarked and began the long trek to the Martello Tower.

Despite the autumnal chill, several bathers splashed and swam in the clear water of the harbour and, further around to the right, the really hardy slithered across boulders and lowered themselves into the freezing depths of the Forty Foot.

Niamh had chosen Joyce's museum as her last port of call.

Before heading for the entrance, she stood for a moment, surveying the sturdy structure of the circular building, its stone a warm yellow in the pale sunshine. She didn't linger downstairs. It was not artefacts she was after, nor memorabilia. She was interested in what the next level had to offer, so up she clambered, laboriously, and with a good deal of difficulty, for she was not a young woman and the stairs were narrow, winding and treacherous. Breathlessly and gratefully she emerged onto the gun-platform. She stood awhile to recover, and then walked the perimeter of the circular floor, once, twice, three times.

She had spent the past eleven days looking in the haunts of her past and in Joyce's *Ulysses* for the key to the nightly sensations that left her saturated with loss. She had completed the dense intricate novel just once, so couldn't claim to have come within spitting distance of unlocking its essence. But she knew this much: she feared for Stephen who would leave Ireland in search of fulfilment and knowledge. Bloom had the good sense to stay put, despite the difficulties of his life. Joyce allowed his Dublin Ulysses to know that it's not the outer turmoil that is the most significant. He allowed him to know that it is our inner demons that need to be conquered, otherwise, regardless of where we wander, these ineluctable fiends will feed on our turmoil, eating away, slowly and inexorably, at our ability to make sense of our lives.

And perhaps the place to most easily conquer ourselves is the place where we are born and raised, the place where we are known best and, paradoxically, least.

Niamh could almost hear W.B. admonish her for speaking of fictional characters as though they were real.

But, ultimately, she found it impossible to separate the man and his works: felt that it was not Joyce's writings alone that would supply her with the answer she needed. The answer was to be found in the writings and in the life as lived because both were so closely entwined. As a young man Joyce had left Ireland and, apart from a few short visits, had remained in exile until his death. But, inwardly, in his head and in his heart, he must have lived for most of those years in his native Dublin. How else could he have produced the vast tomes of *Ulysses* and *Finnegans Wake*?

Niamh looked out over the stretch of the bay: turned to her left and saw the Dublin Mountains, an undulating haze in the distance. Joyce had stood here over a hundred years before. He had gazed out over this very scene, his myopia rendering the vista blurred and indistinct, but despite that, this place and numerous other places in his native Dublin had been engraved on his memory, inscribed on his spirit and he had recalled them in the tranquillity or turmoil of exile and used them as the setting for his groundbreaking writings.

Niamh wanted to emulate Joyce in this particular. She wanted to breathe in the very substance of this place, absorb it through her every pore; have her blood carry it through her veins and arteries so that for the rest of her days it would remain a vibrant, resonant reality: a reality that could be conjured at will, that would be with her as she took her last breath.

As she stood, her eyes glued to the watery landscape, she filled her lungs with the briny air: deeper and deeper she inhaled, until she felt quite light-headed and had to cling to the parapet for support.

*

"While I've been waiting downstairs I could have read the whole of *Ulysses* and made a start on *Finnegans Wake*, not an experience I have any desire to repeat, I can tell you. Have you nearly finished your sentimental journey? I'm famished, not to mention dying of the thirst." Elizabeth's dark head appeared at the top of the stairs, but she did not venture onto the platform. The intrepid woman had no head for heights.

They retraced their steps and lunched at a bistro, patronised by well-heeled young women (if their gear was anything to go by) on Sandycove Road. Niamh opted for the broccoli quiche with a green salad and a glass of sparkling water. Denied her usual coddle, the disgruntled Elizabeth ordered Tuscan stew and a large glass of red.

"*Sláinte!*" Elizabeth raised her glass. "So that's it, that's the end of your meanderings?"

"If you mean, have I finished what I came to do, I think I have."

Elizabeth did not reply immediately. She ate her meal in silence, taking great gulps of wine between mouthfuls. Looking past Niamh to the street outside, she asked in a reflective manner, as though addressing herself, "Now I wonder why it is that emigrants, and Irish emigrants in particular, indulge so happily in the maudlin; the sentimental."

"I wonder why it is that people are so ready to jump to uninformed conclusions," Niamh snapped.

"You must admit that paying a last visit to your native land has more than a touch of the mawkish about it? I can almost hear the violins playing *Come Back to Eirin*."

Niamh signalled to the waitress, paid the bill, left the restaurant and walked quickly towards the station with Elizabeth panting along behind.

*

"I'm sorry," Elizabeth said when they reached the hotel and made the journey upwards in the lift. "I'm sorry if I was a touch insensitive."

"You, insensitive? Never! It's not in your nature." Niamh opened her room door with a flourish and went and sat in the chair by the window. Elizabeth followed and lay on her bed.

Outside the tide was fast approaching the sea wall; the ferry was making its way towards Dublin Port and the sun had begun its slide towards the horizon, sending shafts of crimson light across the surface of the water. Darkness crept slowly around the room until the only light came from a sliver of new moon.

Niamh sat on. The ferry had passed and the virginal moon had disappeared behind a cloud, but she continued to look at the darkened scene, imagining the scurrying of the waves, the fishermen casting their lines into the cold water.

"You're right, of course," she said, at last, to the recumbent Elizabeth. "Emigrants can be a miserable lot, harking back to the past, going on about what they've lost, refusing to acknowledge and value what they've gained, assuming that they have had to bear the most arduous burden."

Niamh hesitated for a moment and then continued. "I came to Dublin to lay a few ghosts, to try to put them to rest. Only trouble was, I didn't know who or what the ghosts were. But thanks to you and Joyce I think I may have nailed the beggars."

She moved from the chair, leaned over the desk and switched on the reading lamp. She looked again into the blackness outside the window and her hand flew to her heart. The shadowy figure of a woman stared back at her. A few seconds passed before she recognized her own reflection.

"You said to take from *Ulysses* what I would, and that's what I've attempted to do. And lo and behold, I've found, hidden in all the complexity of the novel, something so simple, so obvious, I almost missed it." Niamh paused briefly and then continued. "It's about loss," she said. "Loss oozes from the book like water from a bog. Poor Stephen is drenched in it; Leopold almost drowns in it. All loss; nothing but loss." Niamh paused, and then almost in a whisper, she added, "The only thing gained is self-knowledge."

She turned to look at Elizabeth, to find she had been talking to an empty room.

Elizabeth had disappeared.

Done a runner.

*

"I've decided to go to New York."

"More power to you! What made you change your mind?"

Niamh sipped a mouthful of coffee as Elizabeth placed a glass of orange juice and a bowl of fruit on the table and slipped into the chair opposite.

"Oh, I just thought why not. I caught the news last night and it seems the whole world is collapsing — the financial world is in chaos, banks dropping like ninepins, not enough food to feed the world's population, not enough oil for industry and to heat homes, everybody on the make. The suits have brought the world to the edge of destruction so I thought, ah feck it, I might as well break out before we implode: experience one more first before I fall off me horse and am done for."

"I didn't know you liked riding."

"I don't, but I thought you might understand the allusion."

"You'll have to give me time; I'm a bit befuddled with all that's happened."

"I decided I'd give in to W.B.'s pleas and visit his grandma before she expires. So I'll go home to Birmingham, write up my notes, wash my smalls and then off to New York. I've emailed W.B. with the news."

"Maybe Jessica could make it to The Big Apple," Elizabeth suggested.

"Maybe."

"Anyway, I'll come with you. I'm sure I can get someone to fund an academic bash. How about that then?"

Niamh took another mouthful of coffee. "I thought you were confined to barracks, that the police had confiscated your passport."

"All that has changed. I'm free as a bird."

*

It seemed that the young police inspector in charge of the case had been called away to the birth of his first child (or children — it transpired that his wife was carrying twins) and a more experienced officer took his place. In examining the evidence the said officer of mature years, discovered a foil strip containing two Viagra pills that the unfortunate Hubert had not had the opportunity to use. In the interests of collecting still more evidence the diligent public servant expressed his desire to test the efficacy, or otherwise, of the supposedly potent pills and the academic, who had devoted herself throughout her long and illustrious career to collecting and collating evidence (albeit of a literary kind) could not find it in her heart to refuse.

"You what?"

"Sometimes your grammar lets you down rather badly." Elizabeth told the almost speechless Niamh.

"You mean that last night you and that …"

"Detective Inspector."

"You and that man … you …"

"For god sake woman, finish your sentences."

"How could you? Hubert is still warm. I mean …"

"Wouldn't Hubert be the first to applaud? Didn't he believe that life is for living; that after the age of seventy we have a duty to grasp every opportunity with both hands and any other part of the anatomy that might be required and is still functioning? Anyway, Geoffrey has taken the block off my passport and I'm free to travel at will. So when are we off to New York? I would love to be in America when Obama is declared President Elect."

"There's no knowing if he will be.

"I think it was Lowell who wrote, 'The time is ripe and rotten ripe for change; so let it come.' Elizabeth beamed. "I think our time has come at last and I'm only delighted that I've lived long enough to see it. So when are we off to America?"

*

Niamh checked the bathroom, cupboards and wardrobe once more. Apart from her copy of *Ulysses*, which lay on the bedside table, everything was packed. She glanced at her watch: still an hour to go before she needed to vacate her room.

She picked up the book and, hugging it to her, sat on the side of the bed.

She had followed Elizabeth's advice and had taken what was most relevant to her from the text, had found that the work was a hymn to the greatest loss of all — the loss of exile.

It was as simple and as complicated as that.

The Irish had been exiles in their own country for over eight hundred years, had been cast out from their own land; denied participation in its development. For the Irish, exile was not a mere matter of leaving their own country and living elsewhere; the Irish were exiles within their own country, were forced to live outside the mainstream. For them a feeling of exclusion was bred in the bone: for if we cannot belong in the land of our ancestors, the land where we are born, where can we belong?

And Joyce had written it down, had captured all of this in *Ulysses*. He had accepted the one great gift the colonizers had forced on the Irish — the English language — and made it his own. And he told the story of Stephen's internal exile, how his alienation from the Dublin created by hundreds of years of colonization grows as the day progresses and how he is propelled, inexorably, towards the sundering of ties, towards a life of wandering. Bloom's experiences as he walks the streets of the city mirror what might lie in store for Stephen — the slights, the cruelties, the hostilities that are meted out to the stranger. Bloom has the knowledge to teach Stephen, to allow him a glimpse into the future, but Stephen will make his own mistakes. He will learn, as Niamh and all those who had said, "Bad cess to the lot of you," and upped sticks and left, had learned that, in leaving, the problem is compounded. There is no relief to be found in their adopted country, particularly if they seek refuge in the country of their former oppressors. What awaits them is a deeper sense of displacement.

But like Stephen, the young Niamh had rushed headlong towards exile.

She was in love and love would conquer all.

Love had conquered a lot, but by no means all.

And loss will out.

Her loss, the loss that had burst its way into her sleep, screaming for recognition, was the loss of birthright, of a shared history and culture, of the certainty of belonging. Yes, her birthright bequeathed a struggle for identity. Yes, she had inherited a shared history and culture that that had been left in flitters after centuries of occupation. Yes, she belonged to a people who, when she was growing up, did not feel they belonged in their own land never mind anywhere else. Yes, this bag of cats was her troubled heritage and in some ways she had been glad to be rid of it. But it was part of who she was and, yes, despite what she had gained in her adopted country, its loss had weakened the essence of her, had diluted her spirit. It was a loss she had been terrified to confront, for to acknowledge it was to call into question the meaning of her entire adult life.

But she had finally done it. And she was still standing.

And what of the final score?

Returned Exile 1: Demons 0.

Game over?

Possibly.

And she thanked the god she didn't believe in that neither the present or future generations of Irish would suffer this fate. The young Irish had laid the past to rest, had carved out an identity with which they were content and, with the English language to oil the wheels, were confident that they could take on the world, not as suppliants, as had been the case in the past, but as equals.

*

Niamh moved from the bed and stood by the window. She allowed her glance to sweep the bay, attempting to take in every detail. The tide was on its way in and the expanse of wet sand was washed silver by the glare of the autumn sun. As usual, a flock of gulls had taken up residence on a mound opposite her window and she looked at them, mesmerized by their comings and goings. Again and again they soared into the pale sky, painting it with the swirls and circles of their flight before plunging, once again, towards home.

Author's Note

I should like to thank family and friends who shared their knowledge of *Ulysses* and who, during many interesting conversations, helped shape the ideas explored in the book.

Historical dates, names and actual locations were checked on various web sites. Errors that remain are my responsibility.

To order further copies of

NIAMH TAKES ULYSSES HOME

and

GILDED SHADOWS

Please contact:

Tia Publishing
37 Chesterwood Road
Birmingham
B13 0QG

Telephone: +44 (0)121 444 5397

Email: tia.publishing@yahoo.com

Or visit:

www.maryrochford.co.uk

Tia Publishing